Praise for

I0616792

AKM Miles

This is a warm and sexy love story that carries many of the hallmarks of Ms. Miles' writing...I found this to be a sweet and enjoyable read with memorable characters and an emotional storyline ~ *Book Wenches*

Too Keen had a lot of humor in it and it was a very good read to boot...This one is definitely a keeper and a recommend read for readers who enjoy a humorous story with a lot of sex and love in it ~ *Night Owl Reviews*

Fans of author AKM Miles are sure to love this new story and if you have not yet given this author a try, Too Keen is a great book to start off with. ~ *Literary Nymphs Reviews*

Total-E-Bound Publishing books by AKM Miles:

Too Keen
Love, Jamie
Love, Grant

TOO KEEN

AKM MILES

Too Keen
ISBN # # 978-0-85715-063-9
©Copyright AKM Miles 2010
Cover Art by Lyn Taylor ©Copyright March 2010
Edited by Michele Paulin
Total-E-Bound Publishing

Published in 2010 by Total-E-Bound Publishing, Think Tank, Ruston Way, Lincoln, LN6 7FL, United Kingdom.

Total-E-Bound Publishing is an imprint of Total-E-Ntwined Limited.

Manufactured in the USA.

TOO KEEN

Dedication

To Mom (Betty), of course, Angela, Linda, Melanie,
Phoebe, Jan, Kelli, Janet, Alice, Katy,
Chris, Lauren, Devonna, Brian, Beverly, Tehanee,
Marilyn. This is it. The people who know
what I do and support and love me. Love you right
back. Thanks, AKM

Chapter One

"Let me go, you big queer!"

"Make me, ho."

Sandy dissolved into laughter, turned the hose full force on Keen and laughed as he let her go to scramble away. He should have known better. Don't mess with her when she was already in a mood.

"Hey, slut, ease up on the water. We're supposed to be washing the truck, not the hunk."

"You wish. *Homo* hunk. You're wasted around here." She laughed at his expression.

"Got that right. Why couldn't you've been a man?"

"Yeah. And why'd you have to be gay? We'd be so good together, except for those *small* differences." She bent to get the sponge and gave him an eyeful down her shirt, to which he was completely oblivious. She had a generous D-cup chest and small waist. She was one hot babe, and he loved her...for her mind and her humour and her friendship. They were the best of friends and had been for the two years they'd been neighbours.

"Who you callin' small?" he said, bending to scrub the hubcaps. He knew she was thinking, for about the zillionth time, how hot he was. She'd told him enough times that he was built like a brick house. She swore that gays would be lined up around the corner if they knew where he lived. He was supposedly *that hot*. He had a mirror, so he knew he was tall, muscular with broad shoulders. He was strong, tanned, had short blond hair and blue, blue eyes. But Sandy said that they were clear and bright and they shone with honesty and compassion. What the hell? He just didn't see what that was all about. He was a good man. He'd admit to that. He worked on being just that. He chuckled as, once again, she sighed.

"Now what?" He exaggerated his exasperation.

"Just wishing again that you were straight. You need a clone."

"Told you. Got one," he said, scrubbing away. "Name's Kale. Lives and works in Cincy. Not gay, not married, but not interested in settling down either. He lives for his work." He moved around to the next tire.

"You sure? Why don't you invite him down and let me try to change his mind?" she teased him. They'd had this talk before.

"Oh, didn't I tell you, he's coming in this weekend?" he said and waited.

"No way. You butt! You did *not* tell me. How come?"

"There's some kind of shit going on at his job, and he needs to get away. Nashville's out of town so he's coming to visit. Gonna stay with me for about a month, I think. That long enough for you to vamp him?"

"Long enough to try," she said. "If this brother is anything like you, I want to get to know him. I could live in Cincinnati. I'm an emergency room nurse. I could get a job anywhere."

"So, isn't *your* brother still coming in this weekend? Got everything ready for a hungry teenager?" he asked. He'd moved to the last wheel now.

"Step-brother, LJ. Yeah, I guess. I stocked up on burgers and dogs, pop and crunchy things. I'll let him tell me what kind of sweets he likes. Figure all kids like the other stuff. I don't know what Mom was thinking." She shook her head at her mother's request.

"But you don't really mind?"

"Nah. She said he had trouble in his job, which I don't even know about. Just that he needed to get away and change his life. So, Mrs. Cantu is sending her baby to me...for what? I don't know what to do with him. You have to help. No, wait. You can't help. You're gay."

"I'm sorry?" He straightened to look at her, his eyebrows raised so high his forehead was wrinkled.

"I don't mean anything by it, you know I don't. But you can't take him to gay bars or to hang around with your friends."

"Sandy, Miss Slut-Wannabe, you know I don't go to the bars that much and half my friends are straight. It's not like being around me will *turn* him gay. I'm not like the poster boy for 'Come *on*, everybody, be gay like me'."

He had both hands on his hips, in his snug cut-offs, and no shirt. He was hot and sweaty and wet and ripped and, uh-oh, she had that look.

"You, by God, *do* look like the poster boy for joining the gay life. You're the sexiest thing I've ever seen, and as I've told you many times, your body is wasted on men.

Keen's answer was the same each time.

"Not according to them."

Sandy's inelegant snort was her only response.

"Hey, what time is your bro...uh, step-brother, coming in? Maybe we could go to the airport together to get them both. Kale's flight is coming in about eleven-thirty in the morning," he asked, wanting her off the tired subject of his hotness. *Sheesh! Women!*

"LJ's is about an hour before. I don't mind waiting around. I'd love to go together. Make it not quite so awkward for us. I've never even met him." She frowned. "Does that make me a bad sister? When Mom left for Hawaii, neither of us expected her to meet someone, fall in love and marry. She's been back twice, but the kid always had something else to do, so he's new to me. "

"So how does that make you a bad sister?"

Sandy shrugged. "Still amazes me that she went from Nancy Jackson to Nancy Cantu. Angelo Cantu...he's a nice man, and he's crazy about my mom. Mom says the kid is good looking and tall. Evidently, he stands out over there. I hope it goes well. You know how worried I've been that he'll be surly and...like a teenager."

"How old is he?"

"Not sure. He was little when they got married and I guess I just never found out for sure. I guess mid to late teens."

"It'll be okay. If you have trouble with him, I'll take him down a notch or two. We 'bout done here? I'm hot and hungry."

"Damn, do you have to talk like that?"

"What? I just said I was...oh." Keen rolled his eyes.

"Yeah. I'm hot and hungry, too, and you just won't do, sexy as you are."

He swatted her butt on the way into his house where he was fixing lunch for them this time. He was glad he had her to spend time with. She was fun, sassy, easy to get along with and fun to tease.

"Sexy, huh? You becoming a fag hag?"

"Again, you wish."

He'd have swatted her again if she hadn't scuttled out of the way.

"Ha! Too slow." She laughed and headed for his kitchen to help get lunch ready.

Lunch was good, and they ate on his back deck because he had to have the sun. He spent so much time indoors working at his computer for his programming work then running his gym that when he had any chance at all, he preferred to do things outside, thus the high privacy fence around the whole yard.

They checked schedules and made plans to meet on Saturday morning for breakfast and drive out to the airport together. He had a big Suburban he called his truck, so there'd be plenty of room for both of the guys' stuff.

After Sandy left, Keen puttered around. Kale's room was already fixed up for him, and Keen didn't know what he ate these days. He'd figured they'd shop together and fill the pantry and fridge with stuff they both liked then just kick back. He had plenty of help at the gym so he didn't have to be there all the time, and his computer business ran at his pace since he was the owner and only employee.

He'd made a mint off his programmes for security systems for big corporations. His gym brought in a steady income, too, and was growing enough that he and his partner were thinking of opening another in the Brentwood area. He was waiting until after Kale left to worry about all that. He was going to treat this as a sort of vacation himself. He'd check in, but basically, he was on his own.

He wanted his best friend to meet and like his brother. Maybe they *would* hit it off. Couldn't hurt. He knew Kale wasn't happy.

Keen had known something was wrong for about three months. They were identical twins, and they had a sort of...special knowledge about each other. Nothing so concrete as he'd seen on some of the news shows about such things. They couldn't talk to each other in their minds or anything. Sometimes, though, they'd get an image, just a flash, then before long one or the other would call to check on the other one. He'd find out what was bothering Kale so deeply and try to help him deal with it.

Last time had been a gunshot. He'd called and found that Kale's rookie partner had been killed that day. Killed when he jumped in front of Kale to protect him. It had torn Kale up.

Kale had been up for promotion many times, but he'd chosen the streets. He didn't want a more prestigious desk job. He wanted the action and the hands-on feeling of being there, helping out. He'd been kind of lost and out of it since his young partner's death, though. The department was putting him on mandatory leave to see if he could get past it. Now, he'd spend some time with Keen at his gym and seeing the sights in Nashville — whatever it took to get him back on the force and working again. Keen knew he hated doing nothing.

* * * *

Lance Cantu sat on the plane, bored, as they circled the airport, waiting to land. He'd played the games on his laptop so many times, he was tired of them. No challenge.

This trip hadn't been his idea, not that he'd fought it too hard. He just thought that his dad and Nancy really shouldn't have any say in his life. He was twenty-one and could do as he pleased. But they'd been good to him, and he was sort of in limbo right now. He could use the break.

His trouble at work stemmed from two things. He was smarter than his boss, which pissed the man off, and he was gay, which grossed the man out. Since his boss had realised both these facts, he'd been on Lance's case for one thing or another. Lance had gotten blamed for things whether he'd had anything to do with them or not.

The only way to get his parents to relax, after he was fired unfairly, was to agree to come to the mainland for a visit with his step-sister, Sandy. He'd heard nothing but good things about her. He wondered how she'd feel when she found out he was gay and not interested in being there at all? He'd find out soon. The plane was in landing mode. *Finally.*

Chapter Two

Sandy and Keen walked down the concourse towards the waiting area for LJ's flight. She ducked into the ladies room on their way. He walked on, saying he'd wait for her in the seating area. When she was washing her hands, a very, very pregnant young girl came in, crying and holding her stomach. Uh-oh.

Sandy went right into caretaker mode. "Honey, are you okay? How far along are you?"

"I'm due. Like now." She moaned and leaned on the wall, shaking.

"Oh, honey, what are you doing here? Who's your doctor?"

Before the girl could answer, she bent double and screamed. Sandy went right to her and took her arm, easing her down the wall so she was sitting on the floor. She thanked the maintenance gods for having just left the bathroom. It was actually clean. It was cold, too, which kept it from smelling bad. She didn't have time to think about that, or the fact that Keen was going to wonder where she was soon. The girl screamed again and grabbed Sandy's hand, nearly breaking her fingers.

"It's okay, honey. I'm a nurse. Don't worry. You'll be fine. I need to go see if we can get some help."

"No! Don't leave me. I'm so…oh!" The floor beneath the girl was suddenly very wet as her water broke. This baby was coming soon. Lord, help her. Why hadn't anyone else come in? Usually, there were lots of women in bathrooms. Where were they now?

"Okay. It's okay. I won't go. Someone will come in soon. We'll send them for help. Let's see about getting you comfortable." Why did it have to be summer? She was only wearing Capri's and a tank top. No sweater or over shirt to give the girl. Sandy wasn't the wringing hands type, so she just set about doing what she could to make the girl more comfortable. She went to the paper towel dispenser that had thankfully just been filled. There was soap, hot water, and towels, such as they were. She thought about screaming for help herself, but the girl moaned again, and Sandy went back to her.

* * * *

Keen wondered what was keeping Sandy, but he knew nothing about women and their lives so he wasn't about to question how much time she took in the bathroom. Passengers began disembarking from the flight LJ was on, and Keen watched for Sandy's brother. He didn't know what he looked like, so he watched everyone intently.

He noticed a tall, *very* good-looking man standing over to the side. That couldn't be him. He looked much older than a teenager. He seemed pretty…pretty. *Don't even go there*, he told himself. He wasn't here looking for fuck-buddies. He was meeting his own brother and looking for Sandy's.

Keen looked back again, watching for Sandy then walked over to the young man he'd been trying *not* to scope out too closely.

"Uh, are you LJ? Cantu, right? Sandy's brother," Keen asked, as he stood in front of the guy. He was as tall as Keen was and had beautiful dark eyes. His hair was cut short and was silky black. He was really lean and sexy as hell. *Thought you weren't going there...*

"Yeah, Lance. Mom's the only one that calls me LJ. I prefer Lance. Are you Sandy's...boyfriend? I didn't hear that she was *married.*"

"No, definitely not boyfriend. Best friend. I'm...well, not into women. Whoa." He was amazed that those words had just rolled right off is tongue. He watched closely to see if there was a negative reaction. "Not how I usually introduce myself. Sorry, just sort of answering your question." He decided he'd better introduce himself before he scared the guy off and earned Sandy's wrath. "I'm Keen Thomas, Sandy's neighbour. My brother is coming in on a later flight so we came together to pick you both up. I hope you don't mind waiting a few minutes."

"Nope. But, uh, where is she? If she came with you..."

"Stopped at the bathroom and hasn't come out yet. We could go on and get your bags, but she wouldn't know where we were. Wanna just sit for a few, until she comes out?"

"Sure, no prob. What do you do?"

"Computer programming and I'm part owner of a gym."

"Hey, cool. I'm in computers, too. Well, I was before I got canned for being gay." He smiled at Keen. "And for being smarter about computers than the boss."

"So you worked for a homophobic idiot?"

"That's pretty much it in a nutshell." He laughed at Keen's take on it. They looked at each other for a moment, and it was obvious there was interest there.

"Uh, how old are you?" Keen really had to know. He was feeling really pervy looking at Sandy's brother like this.

"Twenty-one. Why? You look funny." Lance turned his head a little, clearly wondering why Keen looked like that.

"Sandy thinks you're in your mid or late teens. I'm just surprised that you're over twenty."

"Can I hope you're pleasantly surprised?" Lance didn't seem to be one for beating around the bush.

"Well, yeah. Actually, I am, but we…uh…should see about your sister. She's been gone a long time. I'm beginning to wonder about her. We can get to know each other and see if we're interested later. Deal?"

"Yeah. That'd be good. Let's go see if she fell in."

When they stood, they realised they were the only two left in the area. As they turned to head back down the hall to the ladies room where he'd left Sandy, they both heard a popping sound. They turned and, as they did, heard a thumping noise behind a door. They looked at each other and both raised their eyebrows. That had sounded like a gunshot. Nah. With all the hoops people had to jump through these days, how could someone get a gun in here?

As one, they headed for the door where they'd heard the noise. If someone was in trouble, they both instinctively wanted to help. Keen cautiously opened the door, and they gasped as they saw one of the security guards bleeding on the floor. Without hesitation, they both hurried over to him to see if they could help. He moaned as they knelt by him, and Keen wished Sandy was there.

"Be…careful…" The guard's voice was shaky. "There's three of 'em. Guns. Mean…and planning something."

"Who? Where are they?" Keen wondered where they'd gone. It was a small room, but then he noticed another door. "Wait, let me see how bad you're hurt. Easy now, let me turn you a little and see if the bullet went out the back. Yes. I believe that's a good thing." His medical knowledge was limited to sprains and such that occurred at the gym.

"Lance, can I have your shirt? I need something to put on the back hole and then something needs to be pressed onto the front. I'll call for help." He took his cell and called 911. The guard reached for it and asked to speak to a cop.

Keen and Lance listened as he told them that there were three men with guns in the airport. The guard wasn't sure what they were doing, but he'd seen them and noticed they were acting oddly, but when he approached, they had grabbed him and dragged him to this office and shot him when he'd reached for his weapon. He didn't know what they were planning, but it had to do with another flight coming in.

The guard started to slur his words, and Keen took the phone. He introduced himself to the officer on the line and asked what they should do. He told them where the guard was and that one of them would stay with him 'til help came. One of them had to go find Sandy. She could sure help here.

They got Stan, the guard, settled as comfortably as possible, and Keen pulled Lance over to the door.

"We have no idea where these guys are and what they want or if they'll hurt anyone else. I need to find Sandy. I have to make sure she's okay, and she could help us out here." He hated not knowing if she was okay. There was too much going on here.

"What do you want me to do?"

"You stay here with Stan until help comes. If I'm not back by then, don't leave here. I don't want to have to look for you. I want you safe. Promise me?" Keen didn't want to face Sandy without Lance in tow, but he felt someone should stay with Stan.

"It's okay. I'll stay with him. Find Sandy, she could maybe help. But hey…"

Lance paused, a little uncertainly.

"What? What is it?" Keen stopped and turned back from the door, not realising that Lance was close behind him. They were suddenly face-to-face.

"Just be careful. I'd like to get to know you much better. Don't let anything happen before I get a taste."

"My, my, aren't you the bold one?" Keen liked it.

"I just know what I like. It doesn't take me long to decide if I want someone."

Keen looked over at Stan, whose eyes were closed. He looked bad. Looking back at Lance, he stepped that little bit closer. And took a quick swipe with his tongue across Lance's full lips. Oh, very nice. Lance's tongue came out to meet his, and Keen gasped. He jerked back, wanting to do the opposite. He wanted, more than he could say, to jerk Lance to him and take a stronger taste. But right, now there were more important things to take care of.

"Hold that thought. And, *you?* Taste fuckin' great." Before he could go any further, he slipped out the door. He really liked Lance. The man was gorgeous, sexy and level-headed. Keen would like to spend time with him. Right now, though, he had to find Sandy and try to avoid three bad guys with guns. Shit.

Keen stepped out and was surprised to find no one in the hallway. He walked on down and headed for the bathroom where he'd left Sandy. Before he got close he felt something sticking into his back.

"What are you doin' in this hall?" a voice asked, right up against the side of his head. "It's supposed to be empty now."

Keen stood still, not wanting whoever had the gun in his back to get antsy. He turned slowly and saw that the guy looked like any other guy. He was expecting a ski mask or something that distinguished him as a bad guy.

"I got separated from my friend. I was just looking for, uh, him." No way did he want to lead this guy to Sandy.

"Well, I think I'd rather you come with me right now. I don't want any loose ends. Too much ridin' on nothin' goin' wrong."

"You call shooting the guard nothing wrong?" Whoa. Probably shouldn't have said that.

"You been snoopin', huh? Well, Dick Tracy, I think I'll take you and put you with him. Keep your mouth shut, or I'll leave you just *like* him."

"No problems, man. I'm no hero. This is *your* show."

"Damn straight. Don't fuck up, and you might live through this."

The guy seemed smug as he pushed Keen in front of him back down the hall he'd come from. He hated that Lance was going to be in the middle of it now.

"Mind telling me what *this* is, exactly?" Keen thought it'd be nice to know what the hell was going on.

"Yeah, right. I'm tellin' *you*. That'd get *me* killed." They got to the door where Lance and the guard were, and Keen paused.

"Uh, this might end up hurting me, but we called for help for the guard. An ambulance and the police should be on their way."

"Shit! *Shit*. Well, that's just *great*. I gotta call Manny. Get in there." He pushed Keen towards the door and turned to pull his cell phone from his pocket. Keen went on into the room and looked for Lance. He saw Stan, who was looking pale and sweaty. As soon as he got in and went to close the door he was grabbed from behind. He turned and nearly clipped Lance on the jaw with his fist. He pulled back just in time and sagged into Lance's arms for a second.

"Shit, man. Sorry. I thought you were one of them." Lance let him go then thought better about it and took him back for a second. Keen put his arms around the younger man and hugged him a moment, enjoying the absence of Lance's shirt.

"Don't worry about it. I'm glad to see you're not freaking out." Keen smiled at him. "Listen, one of them's out there calling a buddy to report that we called the cops. He caught me before I could find Sandy and brought me back here at gunpoint." He took a second to look around the office they were in now.

"Have there been any more here? Wonder where that other door leads? The guard said they have some sort of plan about a plane coming in soon. Weird stuff going on. How did three guys get in an airport with guns in this day and age?"

"Don't know, man. What are we going to do?"

He didn't want anyone hurt. This situation was too volatile. "Exactly what they tell us to, for now. We have to know more. We can't just go off and try stupid heroic stuff. We have to make sure Sandy's all right then, hell, Kale will be walking right into this mess."

"Kale's your brother?"

"Yeah. Identical. Sandy doesn't know that part. I've told her before that I have a brother but all the pictures of us are in my bedroom. I was looking forward to seeing her face when she saw Kale. How's Stan?"

"Not so good. His breathing's getting weaker and he's all pale and sweaty. I don't know what to do for him. I'm good with computers and martial arts, but first aid...not my thing. I feel stupid. I may take a course or something. I hate being ignorant about something—especially now."

"We offer one at the gym. You could take it this summer if you want. I'll give you a discount," Keen said.

"Yeah? Do you teach the CPR? I'll sign up for the mouth to mouth part." Lance evidently wasn't a bit shy when he knew what he wanted.

"No, I'm not the teacher, but I might be willing to help you practice." Actually, Keen wasn't backward in the boldness department, either.

"Oooooh. I should have visited sister Sandy before now."

"Nah. I think now's just about right, if we get out of this in one piece. Head's up, I hear our guy. Be cool. Follow along."

The guy with the gun came in and seemed really pissed so they both kept quiet, waiting to see what he'd do. When he saw Lance, he paused a moment but didn't seem to care one way or the other. He was the one holding the gun.

"You guys are gonna help me. We're gonna go meet a plane and see about our friend."

"You're doing this to meet a friend? Couldn't you just..." Lance trailed off as the guy stepped towards him.

"Yeah, pretty boy, but the Marshal probably wouldn't let us just walk off with his prisoner."

"Oh."

So that explained why they were here, not how they got in. The guy was antsy, walking around the room, looking here and there.

"Uh, can I ask what you're going to do now? The police and ambulance should be here soon, and we told them where the guard was. They'll be coming right here."

"Why, you're being awfully helpful," Gun guy sneered.

"Hey, I just don't want anybody else hurt. If you get caught, it'll be worse for you, the more victims you leave behind. And, frankly, I don't want to be one of them," Keen tried to reason. If the police and medics showed up and they were still there, there'd be questions to answer. This guy didn't seem too willing to be calm.

"Yeah? So? Manny said to take care of this situation and meet him down below. I need you all to come with me. This guy can take his chances, huh?"

Lance spoke up with a question, "What do you want us to do?"

"Just shut up and come on. If you try anything, I won't mind shootin' one of you. Which one, huh? Young guy here or Mr. Helpful? You all know each other? Or hey, maybe, you're a couple." He laughed at his own sick humour.

Keen didn't want him to have *that* to use as ammunition against them so he spoke up.

"No. We just met today." He looked over at Lance and said, "Didn't you say you just flew in today?" He didn't want the man to think they were close. Better to keep it simple.

"Yeah, I was supposed to meet my sister. I just got in from Hawaii."

"Yeah?" the man said. "Always wanted to go there."

He seemed to know his way around the place. They went out of the other door and used back hallways and stairs that the general public never saw. Did the men work here? Is that how they knew the place so well and could sneak guns in? It made sense...as much as any of this made sense. Keen wondered again where Sandy was, and he looked down at his watch to see if Kale's plane was due in yet.

"You got a hot date?" the man asked, leering.

"Nope. Just wondered what time it was. You know this place pretty well. You work here?"

"Once. And it's none of your business. Shut up. We'll meet up with Manny now, and the less talking you do the better your chances for stayin' alive."

Keen snuck a look at Lance and saw he was busy scoping out the place. He was noting the exits and the design of this area of the building. Not a bad idea. Keen took a few seconds to familiarise himself with things. He saw a door up ahead and glanced over. Lance saw him, and when Keen nodded to it and raised his eyebrow, Lance nodded.

All of a sudden, Lance seemed to trip over his own feet and fell right on the floor, ending up right in front of the man. Keen jumped to step over him and fell against the door, secretly putting his hand down to the knob to see if it was locked. It turned. Yes! He let it go and righted himself, watching as the man kicked Lance and told him to get up or get dead. Lance hopped right back up.

"Sorry, man, must've tripped." Lance tried to look embarrassed. He raised his eyebrow at Keen, and Keen nodded. They had one room they knew they could get into if they could get away. Who knew what it was, but maybe there'd be a phone in there.

"What the fuck? Asshole, can't you do anything right? Who are these characters? Why'd you bring them *here*? You know what we'll have to do with 'em now." The guy speaking was the tallest, skinniest man Keen had ever seen. He looked like Ichabod Crane. His long, greasy hair was pulled back in a ponytail, and he was all in black, but his eyes were the lightest grey, seeming almost silver. He almost made Keen shiver. Lance took one step closer to Keen. Yep. Freaked him out, too. Ugly, strange dude.

"Manny, come on. I thought you'd need hostages, and these guys were still snoopin' around in the area, and they saw me so I took 'em. They found the guard I shot and called the police and medic people. They're comin' to get him."

"You're an idiot. I told you what would happen if you messed up again," Manny said and raised his own gun. Without another word, he shot the other man right between the eyes. Keen tried to hold in his gasp, but Lance wasn't able to. His eyes were huge, his face pale, and he just gaped at the man.

"You got anything you want to say, asshole."

"No, sir." Lance was very quiet and very polite.

Keen hoped this man decided he needed them. Obviously, Manny didn't mind killing people. Keen couldn't help it, he stepped up and over a little in front of Lance. Lance was younger, he was Sandy's brother, step or not, and Keen liked him. He felt protective.

"Oh, tough guy, huh?" Manny said, looking at them carefully, probably trying to decide if he might use the younger one against the older one. He turned and yelled, "Derek! Come 'mere. Get this piece of shit out of here. Idiot. Just brought us more trouble…"

He walked off, muttering. Keen and Lance looked at each other. This man was crazy. He'd just shot one of his own men then walked off, leaving them there. Not that they were going anywhere, since he was a little trigger-happy.

Keen looked around. They were in a sort of maintenance bay. There were tools on the far wall, big racks with drawers lining another wall, and a huge empty space in the middle of the room. Nowhere to hide in here.

Sure, there were a lot of possible weapons, but how to get to the other side of the room to get hold of one?

Keen and Lance, together, started backing towards the door they had entered while the other two were occupied with their dead…friend…employee…whatever he had been.

"Hold it, assholes. Where ya goin'?"

"Uh, just away. We don't want any trouble. We don't even know where this is, so…you could let us go, and we wouldn't even be able to tell anyone where you are. Just…just let us go, okay?" Lance had a tremble in his voice, and Keen watched him closely to see if it was real or if he was up to something. Lance cut his eyes to the other side of the big room where Derek dragged the first guy out another door. A gun was tucked in the back of the dead man's pants and Keen wished he could get hold of it.

Lance looked at him and mouthed the words, "On three."

Shit. What was he going to do? Hell, he braced himself for whatever. Lance was closer to Manny, but Keen hated the thought of Lance taking him on.

Suddenly, Lance moved in a blur of motion, and Manny was on the floor, moaning. The gun skittered across the floor. Keen ran for it and scooped it up.

He turned in time to see Manny reach for Lance's leg to try and topple him. Lance danced away and flipped, before coming back to swing his leg and clip Manny's chin, bouncing his head back onto the concrete floor and knocking him out cold.

"Hey! What's going on?" Derek came back in on the other side of the room.

Keen turned and pointed the gun at him and told him, "Come on in, Derek. We were just talking with Manny. He thinks you should come *right* over here. I've got the gun now, and believe it or not, I do know how to use one." He wasn't lying. He used to go practice with Kale when he was first starting his police training.

"What the fuck? Wha'd you do to Manny?" Derek said, his eyes a little buggy.

"Don't worry about him. The gun's on you. That's good, right over here. Lance, get some of that twine over there and let's tie up these two. Damn, man, you're good with those feet," he added.

"Good with my hands, too."

Keen chuckled at the kid's audacity. In the middle of this mess, he was *flirting*?

They tied the two and gagged Derek. Then they headed back up the way they had come. As they got to the office door they'd checked out earlier, Lance stopped. When Keen realised his were the only footsteps in the big hallway, he stopped and turned. Lance stood at the door, one hand on the knob, the other motioning Keen over. The flirtatious look on Lance's face gave away his intentions. No way. Not now. They had to...he found himself walking right over to Lance.

Next thing he knew, they were inside some office, and *he* was up against the door and Lance was halfway down his throat. He grasped Lance in his arms and held him tight. Keen provided the suction to cause Lance to groan and push harder into Keen. Of course, it was adrenaline mixed with relief—and then there was that attraction that had been instantaneous. It all added up to a bruising, thrilling kiss that had them both ready to ignite into flames right there. Hot, wet, thrusting, sucking and even biting to prove they were both okay and were safe in each other's arms.

Lance finally eased up and pulled back just a little, and Keen took the opportunity to push him back then their positions were reversed, and Lance was attacked. Keen thought he took it like a man, a hungry one. Keen wanted more. He wanted hours in bed with Lance. He was so hot and so horny he shook with it. He pushed his hips against Lance's and moaned as their hard cocks bumped and rubbed against each other.

"Keen, more, I need..." Lance wasn't quite coherent. "I can't remember being this way with the few other guys I've been with. I love sex and men, but I've always been selective and didn't screw around with just anybody. But this is different on so many levels."

"I know. I know. Me, too, but we've really got to go. We've gotta, mmm...go. Rather come, huh?" He tried to calm them both. Humour, responsibility, anything he could think of.

"Come, yeah."

"Not now, Lance. Come on, let me go, or I'm going to embarrass myself. It could happen, really. We've got to find Sandy and get the cops and tell them where to find those idiots. I've got to go see if Kale's here yet. Too much to do. But oh God, Lance. You and me, later. It's a date, yeah?"

"Oh yeah. You're Sandy's neighbour, right?"

"Right next door." They smiled at each other and moved to leave the room. They followed the intricate path they'd used before and ended up back by the room where the guard had been. There was now crime scene tape over the door and a couple of officers were inside.

Keen asked, "Is there someone in command here that we could talk to?"

One of the men, Officer Ragan, pointed out towards the main concourse, and they headed that way. Keen walked up to the guy who was obviously the head honcho and told him what had happened. The man immediately called over some men and suggested Lance show them where the guys were while Keen went looking for Sandy…and Kale.

He headed for the bathroom, doubting he would find her there. Some people were gathered around the doorway, and he asked someone what was going on.

"Did you hear? There was a baby born in there. A young girl went into labour, and there was a nurse handy. She delivered it and they just took them to the hospital. Isn't that wonderful?" a lady gushed.

"Do you know if the nurse went with them? She's a friend of mine." Keen looked around at the women standing about. "We were here, and she went into the bathroom. I went on to meet her brother, and now, I can't find *her*."

"She didn't go with them, I know. I saw them leave, and she was still here. I don't know where she went, though. Sorry."

"No problem, I'll find her." He headed towards the area where Kale was due in. He was probably already here. If Sandy went to meet his plane and wait for Keen, she'd already gotten a big surprise. He walked faster, anxious to see both of them then get back to Lance and get out of here.

Chapter Three

Sandy was even more appreciative after the ordeal of birth that the maintenance crew had cleaned recently. She'd used a lot of the towels and soap to clean up then had taken off her shirt and turned it inside out. Not great, but cleaner. She was just glad that it had been a very fast birth or she'd still be in there and might never find LJ.

A crowd had still been around the front of the bathroom, but she'd eased through and headed for where LJ was supposed to have come in. Maybe they were there waiting for her. Nope. Maybe they'd gone to get luggage, she thought, so she headed down there. Nope. Maybe they had already gotten the luggage and had gone to meet Keen's brother's plane. She'd try that next.

She got there and realised that the plane had already unloaded, and she still didn't see Keen or LJ. She looked around, beginning to worry. Where was everybody? Then she saw him, standing in profile to her.

"Keen! Finally! Did you find LJ?" she asked as she hurried up to him. She was so excited she ran her sentences together and gave him no chance to get a word in. "You'll never believe what happened to me. I delivered a baby in the women's restroom. That's why I'm so late. Isn't that cool? A baby girl. She was so tiny and sweet. Mother and baby are fine. Where's LJ? Couldn't you find him? Why aren't you answering me?" She popped him on the arm and stepped squarely in front of him.

"Uh, *who* are you?" he asked.

"Keen, have you lost your mind? Wha' da ya mean, who am I? Duh. You're scaring me. What's up? Has your brother come in yet? Isn't this where he's supposed to be?"

"Do you ever stop talking?"

"What? *What* is your problem? Talk about rude?" What was up with him? He looked pissed and perplexed at the same time.

"Maybe I should introduce myself. I'm Kale Thomas. I take it you didn't know that Keen and I are identical." He smiled down at her, clearly getting it at last. "He loves to do that. So, you don't know where he is?"

"That big shit." She was embarrassed. She'd hit Keen's brother. "You're right, he never told me. Wait 'til I see him. He was gonna have a ball when I saw the two of you together. Stinker."

"So, uh, you delivered a baby. That *is* cool. But I don't know where Keen is."

"Keen and I were going to meet my brother here, too. I stopped in the bathroom, and there was this girl, and things got crazy. When I finally got out, I couldn't find Keen or LJ, and so I thought they might have come to meet you, so I came here. Surprise. So what do you think we should do?" She ran it all together again, embarrassed now at the first impression she must have made.

"Go get my luggage, walk around, maybe have them paged, I guess. Sound like a plan?"

Sandy looked at him intently, then said, "I guess so. Let's go. Man, I gotta tell you, you look just like him. But I guess you know that. He even wore a blue shirt and khakis today, too."

"Yeah, we used to do that all the time — get dressed separately then find out we had on the same things. I'm not surprised he didn't tell you."

"Did you all play tricks on people all the time when you were growing up?" Sandy asked. Knowing Keen, they probably did.

"Some. I grew up a little before he did, but he could usually talk me into things. We were really close, like most twins, I guess. I was a little more serious, and he liked to play," Kale said, with a wry smile.

"He's a hard worker, a great guy and my best friend." Her chin went up a little.

"Hey, I wasn't knocking him. I think he's great, too. Let's go see if we can find him." As they walked towards the luggage area, Sandy could tell he was checking her out, and she liked it. She wished she wasn't wearing a wrong-side-out shirt, for Heaven's sake. *Great first impression*.

* * * *

Finally, after trying several locations and not finding the other two, Keen told Lance they should go out to the truck. Sandy knew where it was and surely she would end up there, hopefully bringing Kale with her. In the interim, he figured he'd use the time to get to know Lance a little better.

They leant on the truck and talked, both trying to hide the fact they wanted to jump the other's bones right there in the parking lot. There was no way to act on their desire, but it was there. They'd been through a lot in a short time, and it had made them more aware of each other and their mutual need.

"You need to distract me, man. I would seriously like to take a big bite out of you right now. I know I'm being forward, but I'm really feeling this...this thing is kinda real. Am I alone here?" Lance managed to sound both eager and hesitant at the same time.

"No way. I'm right with you. Maybe we should get some basics out of the way. Like how far we have to go to be safe, if you really want to go far enough to have to worry about safety, and what you like to do...with a partner, I mean. Think we could get some of those questions out of the way? If — *when* — we get a chance to act on this later, we won't have to waste time on it."

"Good idea. Uh, not necessarily in order, but here goes. I would like to go all the way, several ways, several times. I like it all." Lance didn't have any trouble admitting he liked sex. He smiled at Keen. "Once I realised I liked guys, I actually studied things before I went out and got into the game. I admit for a while it *was* a game to me. I wasn't looking for the big love thing, commitment and all. I tried all kinds of stuff with several guys. It was a definite learning situation." He held a hand up as if to swear before the court. "But, I was always, always safe. I have never gone bareback. That will be saved for when I know it's for real and will last. Something to look forward to, you know?" Lance smiled again, looking intently at Keen.

"I hear that."

"I haven't had a lot of lovers recently. Guess I grew up a little. There's no one now. I decided when I started…well, this part of my life, that I'd get tested every six months, whether I'd been active or not, and I've kept to that. Got my results about two weeks before I left. I'm clean. Got my papers with me. That cover it?" Lance said, leaning in a little, making Keen wonder if this was a good idea, this conversation. It certainly wasn't diffusing the situation.

"Pretty much. I've always been super careful, too. I see too many who have been stupid and find themselves on the cocktail or in the final stages. I like your attitude about safe sex." It said a lot to him that Lance had been smart right off the bat. No chances meant no worries.

"We'll be careful with each other, okay? We'll do whatever we want, but we'll keep our heads on straight. Nothing stupid. I'm kinda anxious to get a taste of you, a real long head to toe taste." Now Keen smiled at the eager look on Lance's face. "I haven't been active in…damn, is it almost a year? Surely not. Hmm, I guess so. I've been diligent with testing, too, and have all my papers in a file. We are both safe, but we'll still stay safe. It's not that I don't believe you…we'll just be smart, okay?" Keen really was a fanatic about safety. He was glad Lance seemed to be, too.

"Well, we've got that all out of the way, but I'm still not distracted, man. Are you sure she'll eventually come out here? I don't want her to be upset that we didn't find her in there. Not the best way to start out this trip. I'm suddenly real interested in staying awhile. Tell me what she's like?"

"Sandy's the best. We've been friends since she moved in next door. She's a nurse in the emergency room at the hospital nearby. She has weird shifts, but we share a few chores back and forth." He stood up and motioned for Lance to join him. He couldn't be stationary any longer. At least, they could walk around the area. He went on with his description of Sandy. "She'll do some of the things for me that I don't particularly like, and I'll do the heavy labour stuff for her. She's mostly self-sufficient. We just use it as excuses to get together. We go out together when neither of us has anyone else around at the time. She's cool with my life. She'll be cool with you, too. She know you're gay?"

"Nope. Didn't come up. I'll certainly tell her, though. I want to be able to come and go as I please, like maybe next door. So, she'll have to know. That cool with you?" Lance glanced over at Keen.

"Hell, yeah, sooner the better as far as I'm concerned. By the way, we've got to go down to police headquarters tomorrow to finish talking to them. I'll take you if you want."

"Do I want you to take me?" Lance deliberately mistook the question for more than it was. "Oh, yeah. How 'bout you? You take it?"

"Yeah, if it's right, you know?" Keen didn't even act like he didn't catch the double meaning. "Sometimes it just isn't what I want. I think I'd like to try pretty much all of it with you. Sandy better hurry up. I'm getting more turned on by the minute. I've been without any for too long a time. I'm ready to make up for lost time, and I like it that I'm getting to know you." Speaking of getting to know about him... "By the way, you scared the shit out of me in there. I didn't know what you were going to do. I was afraid you were going to get hurt or killed and I'd have to tell Sandy. You're something else, really good. Have you done competitions?"

"I did when I was younger. Went all the way to the top. I've kept it up and will look for a place to practice here, but I don't compete anymore. You know a good place?"

"Yeah, just down the street from our gym. I'll show you. I gotta tell you, Lance, I'm glad you decided to visit your sister."

"Me, too, Keen."

"Keen! Hey, oh my God, you're not going to believe…" Sandy hit his arm and then hit it again.

"Ow!"

"You shit. You could have told me you had a double. Where have you been? We've looked everywhere. Why didn't you come find me? Oh, where's LJ? This isn't…*is it*?" Her voice got higher as she shut up and looked at Lance.

"Hey," Lance said, grinning.

"LJ? Hi, welcome to Nashville. I hope you like it here. I can't believe I missed your plane. I'm so sorry. I went to the bathroom and ended up delivering a baby."

"No shit?" Keen said, smiling through his pride in her. Then he, too, realised he had someone else to see. "Kale! Hey, glad you're here. I see you found Sandy. Uh, we've got sort of an adventure to share with you all, too. What do you say we get all the stuff in the truck and head out? Let's stop and eat somewhere and swap stories."

Kale and Sandy tried to get them to tell all, but he and Lance said they wanted to wait until they stopped to explain everything. Keen encouraged Sandy to expound on her adventure in the women's restroom until they stopped for a meal. Soon, they sat around a table at one of the great steak houses close to Keen and Sandy's homes, all amazed at what they were hearing.

Kale said, "You know, there *was* a Marshal with a prisoner on the plane with us. I didn't pay too much attention to it, though. They sat in the back. Damn, Keen, leave it to you to get caught up in the middle of a crime scene."

"Yeah, it should have been you," Keen agreed. "You'd have known more about what to do. You're the expert at this kind of thing. We were kind flying by the seats of our pants, no pun intended. It really could have ended badly. Manny was a freak, man. No expression at all when he shot that guy right in front of us. Don't think he was too smart, though, huh Lance?" Keen said, looking over at Lance for confirmation, trying to downplay it a little so Sandy wouldn't be too concerned.

Sandy had grown pale as they told what had happened to them. She looked from Keen to Lance and made an obvious effort to not show how worried she really was.

Kale came in with an attempt at calming her down. "It sounds like they had it under control. I think both of our brothers are pretty clever and talented. Just don't make a habit of getting into these situations, okay, you two?" He had started out reassuring Sandy and ended up teasing the two other men.

Sandy said, "LJ, I never knew all that about you, a champion in martial arts and then the computer stuff. You should talk to Keen. He's in computers, too. You all might have a lot to talk about. Give you something to do when I'm working. What? Y'all are looking funny? What did I miss?" She looked back and forth between them.

Keen wasn't saying anything. It was up to Lance when he told Sandy about being gay. He might be hesitating because of Kale. Probably, Lance would rather discuss it with his sister in private. Keen knew that Sandy wouldn't have a problem with it, but Lance had only just met her.

They talked more, enjoyed the dinner and headed for home. The talk continued with Lance telling about his boss's firing him.

"The truth is I caught the man in too many mistakes, and I had to save the day more than once. The boss didn't like being shown up, so he found a reason to fire me."

They all commiserated with him and asked if he planned on getting another job in the same area.

"I'm not sure where I'll end up, but I'd like to thank you, Sandy, for this chance to take some time to figure things out."

"No problem. We're family even though we've never met. I have to say you're a very good-looking, young man. You probably have to beat the girls off with a stick. Maybe you'll meet someone here to go out with. I hope you aren't too bored here." Sandy looked worried all of a sudden.

"Don't worry. Keen says he has a gym, and he knows a place where I can practice. I think I'll find plenty to do. Don't worry about me." Lance wouldn't look at Keen. He probably thought he'd lose it and blush or stutter or burst out laughing. He'd find plenty to do all right. Keen would see to that.

"So what do you and Kale have planned, Keen Dale?" Sandy asked, laughing when he frowned at her use of his whole name.

"Watch it," he threatened her.

"What? I think it's cute."

From the back seat, Kale spoke up, "You didn't..."

"She's like the Gestapo, man. She has ways of making you talk. She knows the whole sordid tale."

"What're you all talking about?" Lance spoke up this time.

"Oh, it's just their names. They're so cute. Keen Dale and Kale Deen. Their mother had a sense of humour."

"Thanks, Keen." Kale said, not really sounding mad.

"Hey, you're a cop. Maybe you'd have a better chance with her. I can't seem to keep a secret around her. She's relentless."

"So you were the KD's, huh?" Lance spoke up, taking the heat off Sandy.

"Actually we were called the Kuh-duh's. Whatever. Someone said it, something about phonics, and it caught on."

"Speaking of names, Sandy, your mom is the only one who calls me LJ. I really *do* prefer Lance, if you don't mind."

"Of course not, honey. I'm sorry. It's all I've ever heard you called. You look like a Lance. I'll try to remember," Sandy told him, clearly glad he'd felt comfortable enough to tell her.

"No problem. I won't freak if you forget. Is there anything I can do to help you out while I'm here?"

Keen hoped Lance really liked what he'd seen of Sandy so far. He now had a vested interest in wanting her to like Lance and let him stay, maybe longer than planned.

When they got home Keen and Kale gathered Kale's luggage and headed for their place. Lance got his bags and headed into Sandy's. Before each of them went in, Lance glanced across to find Keen glancing at him, and they both smiled. They'd see each other soon. It was unspoken but there between them.

Chapter Four

Kale had been impressed last night with Keen's workout room. They had both worked up quite a sweat as they'd gone through each machine and even did a little easy sparring on the mat. When Keen got them both a sports drink and some towels, they sat on a couple of benches that were against one wall.

"I know something happened at work, something bad. You don't have to tell me, but you know if you need anything…" Keen started, as they both opened their drinks.

"I know. I just…it's hard, Kee. My partner's dead, and I'm directly responsible." Kale's voice shook as he spilled his pain.

"There's no way I believe that. Tell me what happened. When was it? Did you have to do all that counselling stuff? Do your superiors think you were responsible?" Keen knew it wasn't possible that Kale had done something to get his partner killed. He went ruthlessly by the book. He often trained rookies because he was so good at what he did.

"We weren't even at a crime scene. We'd stopped to get some snacks and drinks at a little convenience store. I came around a corner and met him at the end of the aisle. He turned and saw something and jumped in front of me. Next thing I knew, I heard gunfire and he was down. I swung around, drew and shot the guy before he could get off another round. There were people in there, Keen, kids and mothers, and this guy was just shooting. What the hell? Who does that?"

"So what was wrong in what you did?"

"I was supposed to be teaching him, helping him, not the other way around. If I'd been paying more attention maybe I'd have seen the gunman first." Kale rubbed his forehead, pressing in hard as if he could force the memories out of there.

"Oh, come on. You probably saved countless people by taking him out. You had no way of knowing."

"Rodney jumped over and took a bullet for me. He wasn't married, but he had a steady girlfriend, and she was devastated. Keen, I would never want anyone to die for me. I'll never forget his face as he lay there dying." Kale had tears in his eyes now.

Keen put down his drink and didn't think twice about putting his arms around Kale. How long had it been since he'd hugged him like this? Since they were kids?

"Listen to me. I know I don't have the training to say the right thing here, but I know you. Your partner, Rodney, acted on instinct that day. Probably instincts you helped instil in him. He acted naturally for him, saving the life of someone. It's what you all are trained to do." Keen put his hand on Kale's head, rubbing a little as he talked. "The fact that it was you, a man he probably looked up to, made his death an act of honour. Don't take that away from him by thinking this was your fault. If the tables were turned and you'd seen the guy first, I'm sure I'd be a sad and bereft man right now. Honour him, Kale, by going on and working with others like you did him and teaching them to love the job like you do."

Kale sobbed once then drew a few big deep breaths. Kale had listened to what he'd been saying, Keen knew, from the silent stillness Kale had exhibited while Keen had been talking. Keen didn't know where the words had come from, but he knew he was right. He hoped Kale would be able to reconcile himself to the harsh reality he faced.

"You'd make a pretty good shrink. A lot of what you said is true. He did act instinctively. He was a good kid, a good officer. I guess I lost it a little. I went through the mandatory counselling, but just couldn't get back into things. Too many memories, and too much raw pain. I needed a break, and my captain knew it. I'm on mandatory leave. I've got a month with leave time and vacation time. I hope that's okay with you." Kale drew back, patting Keen's shoulder, in what Keen knew was an acknowledgement of what Keen had done for him. It was enough.

"I'm thrilled to have you here. With Lance visiting Sandy, too, we can all do some sightseeing. There are lots of interesting things to see and do in Nashville, believe me. Maybe you'll like it so much you'll want to stay. They have a police force here, too, you know." Keen knew it would be a continuing struggle for Kale. His words of wisdom might have helped a little, with the added benefit of Kale's being able to break down and lose it with Keen there for support. Kale would take the time he needed to heal, but he was on the way. Keen was very proud of his brother, very proud, and damned happy that Kale was alive and right there with him. That situation could have gone the other way and he'd be the one needing a shoulder.

"One thing at a time, Kee. Let's get my head straight first. Then at least one of us will be straight." Kale tried to make a joke.

Knowing it was for his benefit, Keen let him get away with the weak jab.

"Funny, Ka. Let's hit the showers and find something for supper."

The rest of the evening passed with them talking about anything but work and pain. Kale got in a few more teasing remarks about Keen having already fallen for Lance. Had they been that obvious? Keen kept suggesting that Kale find some time to get to know Sandy a little better. He honestly did think they would get along well together.

* * * *

After breakfast, Keen had an appointment with Lance at the police station first. There were forms to fill out. They had both agreed to go down there since they wanted Manny and Derek to get the maximum sentence. Keen also meant to check on Stan, the guard. He was going over to pick Lance up.

"So, what did you think of Sandy?"

"Why you wanna know? Don't start that again, Keen," Kale said.

"I don't have to. She's been asking me for almost two years if there were any more like me anywhere. She loves me, but alas, it's not to be. Now you, on the other hand, not gay, not married, not doing anything else for a while. Why don't you take her out? She's a great woman. You could do worse."

"I'm not looking to do at all, Kee. You know that."

"Well, Ka, you don't have to be looking to find, you know. Just don't throw out the idea. Besides, I want to spend some time with Lance, and if you keep Sandy busy, we'll have some time together."

"So now I'm here to cover for you, huh?

"Yeah, pretty much. We really hit it off. I'd like to see where it could go. I'm into him in a big way."

"Ha! You'd like to be."

"That, too." They laughed as Keen left to go pick up Lance.

Keen and Sandy had talked, and he knew she was taking a few days off to spend some time with Lance. He noticed that her car was missing, though, and wondered where she was. Had Lance forgotten their appointment? He knocked on the door and waited.

Suddenly, the door was wrenched open. His hand was taken and he was pulled inside. He laughed at Lance as the door was slammed and locked. He found himself up against it with Lance in his arms. Somebody was eager...and very, very hard.

"Tell me I'm not the only one who feels like this," Lance pleaded, right before he pressed his open mouth over Keen's. Keen would have told him he wasn't alone in his desire, but he set about showing him instead. He was familiar with Sandy's place so he walked them both towards the living room couch, without losing the lip lock.

He turned so he was sitting on the back of the couch and pulling Lance into his arms. Keen spread his legs so they fit together very tightly. Lance was quick to move against him, not in a smooth rhythm, but rapidly, raggedly, obviously in need.

Keen put his hands on Lance's ass and pulled him even closer, moving him around, mashing their hard cocks together, creating the much needed friction. Lance groaned into his mouth and tightened his arms around Keen's neck.

He pulled back and mumbled, "I'm sorry. I'm kind of dopey. Too many time zones yesterday. I didn't sleep too well. I just…I thought about you…us…all night…and…"

"Not a problem, Lance. I feel the same way. I thought about you, too. Come back here and give me that tongue again."

Lance pulled his head back a little and said, "You like kissing? I mean, I know we did yesterday, but most guys…I mean…"

"Everybody's different, Lance. Me, I love kissing. Always have. You don't?"

"Yeah, I mean, yeah, I do…love it. I just thought most guys thought it was, you know, not cool."

"I love the way it feels. A soft, wet tongue moving in my mouth. I love it soft and light and easy, and I like it rough and hard and strong. Kind of like sex. I like it both ways, you know. There's a time for both. How about you? You only like it one way, or are you into experimenting and doing it as many ways as we can think up?"

Lance didn't answer him just pressed his open mouth back to Keen's. He slid his tongue in and moved it in and out, just like he was fucking Keen's mouth. Keen provided a nice suction, and they kept it up, both making sweet moaning noises as it got hotter and hotter.

Keen kneaded the round globes of Lance's ass and ground Lance's groin against his own. Now they had a smooth rhythm going. They pushed against each other repeatedly and groaned as each got closer and closer to…

"Stop. God. You are something else. Give me a second," Keen said against Lance's neck as he tried to calm his pounding heart and will his dick to stop trying to push its way through the zipper of his jeans. Ouch. He stroked the back of Lance's head as he tried to ease them both down from their sexual high. This kid had him in knots. He had to stop this. They had to take care of business.

"Where's Sandy?" he finally managed.

"Gone to the grocery. She's cool, like you said. I like her. Uh, is she going to freak when she finds out I'm gay? And, if we, you know, is she gonna go ballistic? I don't want to come between you." He shrugged his shoulders. It was obvious he was uncomfortable thinking he could ruin the friendship between Sandy and Keen. "I know you all are great friends. She told me how much she likes you and how much you help her."

"I don't think your being gay will freak her out. She's pretty together about things like that. But I don't know if she'll like us being together. Could go either way." He matched Lance's shrug, not really sure. "She could be cool with it, her brother and her best friend getting together. Or she could think I was a sleaze for seducing her baby brother."

"You didn't…hell, I came on to you first. It's not like I'm, you know, the kid she thought I was," Lance said.

"Yeah, well, we'll just play it by ear. See how she does. We talked about doing some things together. I'll see if she wants to cook out over at my place tonight, and we'll see what's what. It's up to you whether you tell her before then or not. Let's go get this police stuff done so we can get back to normal."

"I don't know about you, but this is better than normal for me. I've got this feeling of great..." Lance paused looking for words, and Keen supplied it for him.

"Anticipation?"

"Exactly. I really want to be with you."

"We'll find ways. I need to spend time with Kale, and you need to get to know your sister. But we'll find time for each other. Now, let's get out of here, or I'll end up fucking you over the back of this couch, and Sandy won't have to wonder about you. Not really the way you should come out to her." Keen gave him a squeeze.

They straightened up and went to the station to do their duty, filling out forms and answering questions. They asked about the guard and found that he had gone through surgery and would recover, after a long rehabilitation. They left the precinct after a long two hours or so, and Keen called Sandy to see if she wanted Lance home or if he should get them some lunch. She had already had hers, so the two of them decided to grab something on the way home.

They went through a fast-food drive-thru for burgers and fries, and they sat in the parking lot and talked more. Keen revealed he was a very good cook, and Lance said he was great at doing dishes. They laughed then Lance said he could cook the basics and would like to learn more.

"Sports?" Lance asked.

"I like baseball and basketball. Don't really care for football that much. You?" Keen fired back.

"You'll think it's weird, but I like to watch figure skating. The men's competition. The idea of flying around the ice and soaring up in the jumps like that is really cool to me," Lance admitted, looking like he thought maybe Keen would make fun of him.

"I can see where that would intrigue you. There's a rink here. Have you ever skated? We could go," Keen offered.

"No, I haven't. I might break a leg, but I'd like to try it at least once," Lance said, eagerly.

"I imagine you'd try most anything at least once. I like that about you. You're fearless, aren't you?"

"Pretty much, yeah. What about music? Don't tell me you like country just cause you live in Nashville," Lance said, wincing, his thoughts on it obvious.

"Hey, where's that open mind I've noticed about you? I think I can introduce you to some good country music that you'd really like. I plan on taking you to a couple of bars and getting in some dancing, too. Trust me, you'll like it."

"With you, I don't doubt it a bit. Count me in." Lance sounded eager to experience anything Keen wanted to show him.

Nothing was mentioned about the need building in each of them as they spent more time together. Keen tried not to get caught up in glances between them and the aborted attempts to reach out to each other. They weren't in the right place or time. Soon, though, Keen promised himself.

* * * *

It was a very strange day for Sandy. Lance came back from the meeting with the police looking very solemn and asked if he could talk to her. They grabbed drinks and went out back to sit on her patio.

"I want to tell you something, but I don't know how you'll take it."

"Lance, what's the matter? Is there something wrong with Mom, or are you unhappy here or...?" He had her worried with his hesitant expression.

"No. It's nothing like that. It's...um...I'm gay." He just left it out there for her to take it however she wanted.

"Oh. Oh...really? Well, honey, I don't know what you expected, but you have to know it doesn't make any difference to me. My best friend in the world is gay. Does Mom and your dad know?" Something suddenly occurred to her. "Are they okay with it? Is that why you're here? Did they give you a hard time?"

"No, they're okay with it. They've known awhile. It, well, it's part of the reason I got fired from my job. Oh, it wasn't said — he could've gotten in trouble for that — but it was obvious. Anyway, I wanted out of there, needed a big change. Your mom suggested I come over here for a while. I didn't think it was fair to keep secrets from you since you're letting me stay here."

"Hey. Either way is fine. I'm glad you felt like you could tell me. I think we're going to get along fine. You don't have anything to worry about, okay?" She really was comfortable with Lance's being gay.

"There's more."

"More?"

"Yeah, uh, Keen and I, well, we sorta..."

"No way. Already? He didn't try to...no, he wouldn't..." She was a little confused. She wasn't sure how she felt about this development.

"No way. Don't even think that. I'm the one who hit on him first. Does it bother you? Are you mad?"

Poor Lance, she thought, he probably didn't feel they had a good enough rapport yet to know how she was feeling.

"You know, I don't know. I'm certainly not mad. I've had to change my thinking about you already when I found out you were twenty-one. Lance, that puts you in the do-whatever-you-want category." She smiled at his relieved expression. "I'm your sister, not your keeper. You're old enough to make your own decisions and your own choices. I love Keen. He's a wonderful man and a great friend. I couldn't think of a better person for you to become involved with. So, I guess I just answered the question, huh? I just had to say it. I really am okay with the idea." The more she thought about it the easier it was to…think about.

"Cool. He mentioned something about having a cookout over there tonight. Is there anything you want me to do? Can I help?"

"Let's go over there and see what he has planned, and we'll know what we need to bring. How's that?" She laughed when his face lit up at the mention of going over to see Keen.

"You're gone on him already, aren't you?"

Lance blushed and had to admit, "Yeah. He's pretty cool. He seems like a really nice man. He was great yesterday with those guys, and well…he's pretty hot."

"You're telling me. I've been bitching at him for two years for being gay. He's gorgeous and built like a dream and unbelievably nice." She laughed up at him and teased a little. "Damn. After all this time, I have to hand him over to you. There is no justice in the world."

"Hey, he's got an identical twin who's not gay. Go after him."

"The subject has been discussed. Kale doesn't seem too interested, though."

"Why not? You're a total hottie."

"Why, thank you, little brother." She laughed as he blushed again.

* * * *

Keen answered the door, and his face lit up when he saw his visitors.

"Hey, what's up?"

"Lance says we're having a cookout tonight. I want to see what we're supposed to bring. What time, too?"

"Come on in. Kale and I were working out. Lance, you wanna go see my home gym?"

"Yeah, that'd be cool." He followed Keen to a room on the left that had a mat in the middle and some equipment to the sides. Nice stuff. Lance seemed more interested in the mat.

"Can I use the mat?" he asked, excited. "It's big enough for me to work out on. I need to get some practice in. I've been without for a few days, and I really want to loosen up.

"Sure. Kale, it won't bother you if Lance uses the mat, will it?" Keen asked. Kale was on the treadmill, and it looked like he had been for a while.

"Not at all. Knock yourself out. I'll watch," Kale said, taking a towel and wiping his face while he continued with his run.

Lance took off his shoes and headed for the mat, his face intent as if already planning a few moves in his mind. Keen went back to Sandy. He wondered if Lance had told her.

She punched him, hard, when he got back to the living room.

"Ow! Again! What was that for?"

"You got something you want to tell me?" She acted like she was mad, but she wasn't that good at it.

"Uh, I don't know."

"You and Lance?" She prompted him.

"He told you then?" he asked, looking a little sheepish, as much as he could anyway. He was a grown man and didn't do sheepish very well.

She relented and hugged him while she laughed up at him.

"Yeah, he was afraid I'd be mad. Not. It's not fair, though. I guess he's gonna be spending a lot of time over here."

"Not if it bothers you at all, Sandy. Really."

"It doesn't. You know I'm cool with it. And, he's a grown man. I can't believe I was so off on his age. I should have kept up better with that. I feel stupid that I didn't even know how old my brother is."

"It's not like you ever knew him. He's pretty special, though. He's fantastic with the martial arts stuff, and I'm anxious to see what he can do with a computer."

"That's not all you're anxious to see, I bet."

"There is that," he agreed and laughed with her. All was going to be okay. Whew! "Let's plan this thing tonight. What were you all going to do the rest of the day?"

"Nothing. What about you two?"

"Same. Wanna just hang out here and get to know each other? You and Kale might hit it off if you spent a little time together."

"Don't embarrass me, homo." Sandy swatted him.

"Not likely, slut," he threw back at her. He loved her and would love for Kale to see in her what he did.

They went to the home gym and stood at the door, watching Lance. Kale had stopped on the treadmill and just stood, watching. It was as if they were at an exhibition.

Lance was totally unaware of his audience. He moved across the mat in the most graceful display of skill Keen had ever seen. This kid...this man was spectacular. Keen stood, entranced. They watched for a long time, no one wanting Lance to stop. He twisted and turned and leapt and kicked. He landed lightly and sprang up again, turning and flipping to land again. Pure grace. He finally settled, and all three applauded.

Lance jerked as if just realising anyone else was there. He turned red when he saw they all watched him.

"Lance, my God, you're wonderful. I've never seen anything like that. I'm just amazed." Sandy went to him to hug him and he stepped back.

"I'm all sweaty..."

"I don't care. Come here, I'm so glad I saw that." She embraced him anyway, and he looked over her shoulder at Keen and raised his eyebrows. Keen raised a thumb to show him all was okay with them. He relaxed into her hug.

Keen and Kale said simultaneously, "That was awesome."

Everyone laugh at the twin thing. The four of them were now divided into Kale and Keen and Sandy and Lance. Keen decided he wanted to change the pairings so he went towards Lance. Sandy stepped back and turned towards Kale as she apparently noticed the look Keen gave her brother.

"It's getting hot in herre..." she teased, quoting a favourite song.

Keen was looking at a sweaty, flushed Lance and thinking about the next line. The one about taking off all your clothes. Not what he should be thinking about with Sandy right there! Time to redirect, he thought.

"Hey, there's a guy who has a dojo close to my gym. Would you like to check it out? You could probably get a better workout there. You could even see about getting a job, if you're interested. You certainly have the talent," Keen said, his eyes again roaming over Lance in an approving manner.

"Thanks. That could work. I'd like to meet him, see his place. That was great. I've been missing that. I'd like to practice more. Can I...I mean, is it okay to...?" Lance glanced from Keen to Kale and back as he asked the question.

Keen was quick to answer. "Come over and practice on the mats? Sure. Anytime. I'll get you a key, and you can come and go as you please. Hell, Sandy does — well, she always knocks first. You can just come in and make yourself at home."

He looked at Kale and Sandy then Lance and asked, "Want a quick tour? Then you can go shower and change. We're gonna hang out here this afternoon then cook out later." He turned and Lance followed him out of the room, leaving Kale and Sandy standing there, awkwardly.

"That was subtle, huh?" Sandy said.

"That's Keen."

"Listen, don't feel like you have to entertain me. Go on and take a shower. I know my way around here. I'll go to the kitchen and see what he's planning for tonight then I'll know what to add to it."

"Thanks, I do need to clean up. I'll meet you there, and we'll check it out together. I'd be glad to help you fix whatever. I have a feeling we might be on our own this afternoon, and I don't mind that, really."

"Uh, okay. See you." She found herself blushing now and left for Keen's kitchen. She felt a little funny, thinking about Keen and Lance somewhere in the house, doing who knew what.

She hadn't really thought about what gay men did, she just knew she loved Keen and didn't care that he was into guys. But with Lance in the picture and interested in Keen, she had the situation kind of in her face, so to speak. She just wouldn't think about it.

She puttered around in the kitchen, looking in the refrigerator and freezer to get an idea what Keen planned for supper. She saw a package of good steaks, found baking potatoes and the makings for salad. Looked as if she was doing dessert. Maybe she and Kale could go over to her house and cook something up. And didn't that just sound delicious?

"Behave yourself, girl," she admonished herself.

"Oh, now what's the fun in that?"

She yelped and jumped. Kale stood behind her, looking more delicious than anything she could fix in her kitchen.

"You scared me. You were very quick and quiet." She laughed at herself.

"I'm usually on the run. Sorry. What's the plan?"

"Keen has everything except dessert so I thought maybe we could go over to my house and make something up for that. Maybe leave them a note. I don't know where they went, but I'm not gonna go lookin'." She blushed again.

"I heard them on the patio while ago. I'll tell them we're going over there, and we'll be back at…say six? That give us time to whip up something sweet?" He smiled at her red face.

"Sweet, yeah."

"Relax. I'm not gonna jump you," he assured her.

"Darn it." She might blush, but she wasn't stupid. They laughed together, and he slipped out to tell Keen and Lance they had the house to themselves for the rest of the afternoon.

Kale found them in the hall beside Keen's room. Keen had Lance up against the wall, and it looked like they might need to take it on inside the room.

He cleared his throat and had to fight a laugh as they sprang apart.

"Chill. Sandy and I are going next door to make something for dessert. We'll be back about six. That work for you all?" He didn't even wait to see what they said. He heard the bedroom door close before he reached the other end of the hall. Evidently, it worked for them.

* * * *

"I like your brother," Lance said as he stepped into the room and reached for the bottom of his shirt to whip it over his head. "Still need a shower, man."

"Not a problem. Want some help?"

Lance's eyes widened then he grinned and nodded. Keen went to him and helped divest him of the rest of his clothes. He followed suit then they stood in front of each other, staring...and smiling. Keen certainly liked what he saw and hoped Lance felt the same way.

"God, you are just sex walking." Lance didn't even try to keep the appreciation from his voice. He eyed Keen up and down and back, finally stopping in the middle as his eyes widened. "Wow," he said, sounding reverent.

"Me? You're so tall and lean and strong. You have sleek, ropy muscles and your skin is such a gorgeous colour."

"Thanks to Dad."

"For such a thin man, you are, uh, incredibly...incredible." Keen smiled and reached out for Lance, who laughed and sidestepped.

"Shower, sweaty, stinky...please. I don't want our first time to be...not so good. I want it to be so good, Keen."

"Follow me. I'll make sure you're squeaky clean then we'll make sure the first time is...so good."

When Keen had moved into this house he'd done a little remodelling in the master bathroom. He'd done the oh so gay thing and had a big glass shower with multiple jets and benches around three sides. There were shelves, which were well-stocked, not that the stuff had been used lately, but he was glad now he'd gone to the trouble.

"Wow. This is nice. Fire this thing up, Keen, and let's get wet."

Keen did just that, and soon they were enclosed in the glass box with water everywhere. He grabbed the shampoo and went for Lance's hair, rubbing and scratching his head then moving him into the spray to rinse. Keen went ahead and did his own hair in record time. Then he grabbed the soap and lathered his hands, but this time, he took a little more time. He moved his hands from Lance's shoulders down his arms then up and under them. He looked right into Lance's eyes as his hands scrubbed his pits, causing him to raise them up so Keen could reach him better.

Lance loved the care and attention. Yes, he was desperate for sex with Keen, but he'd never had anyone bathe him before. Fuckin' cool. He turned when Keen nudged him. He dropped his head and nearly melted into the floor as Keen massaged his neck and shoulders then on down his back. Keen took special care cleaning his buttocks and the crack between. He spread his legs, giving Keen room to reach whatever he wanted to reach.

He gasped as Keen soaped and explored his heavy balls. He shuddered and pushed back, wanting more. Keen's other hand reached around and took hold of his hard, leaking cock and with only two or three strong pulls had him shooting his load against the glass wall. He jerked a couple more times then relaxed back into Keen's waiting arms. He turned and took Keen's head in his hands and opened his mouth over Keen's. He wanted to inhale him.

The shower was steamy and smelled of soap and sex and hungry men. Lance had his hands on his dream come true. He pushed his tongue in and raked it across Keen's teeth then engaged his tongue in a mighty duel. He stepped into Keen's body and moaned as they seemed to meld together. The heat in the shower and the warmth of their skin had them nearly adhered to each other.

"Feels so good…Keen…want you…want you to fuck me…fuck you…suck you so good, taste you, lick you all over. Come on, we done here?"

"Hell, yeah. Come on. We'll play in here some other time. Race you to the bed."

"But we're wet." Lance paused.

"We'll dry, I promise. The heat will take care of that. I'm about to go up in flames right now. Touch me, and I'm gone."

They hit the bed at the same time and rolled together, laughing. They ended up facing each other, and Lance had to say, "You are the hottest, sexiest, most beautiful man I've ever known. I can't believe you're interested in me."

"Believe it. Right back at ya. You make me want—and not just sex. You make me want to experience things more.

Touch more, taste more, take more time to know you. Am I making sense?"

"Yeah. Feels different. Better, more intense, real. Like this could really be something special. Enough of that, though. We'll explore feelings later. Now, I want at that body. My turn, yeah?"

"I'm yours to play with, Lance. Just do it now." Keen was so hard he was hurting. He sighed then moaned as Lance moved down to his groin and took his rock-hard cock in his hand then into that pretty mouth. Oh, heat. Wet. Soft. Suction. A quickly fluttering tongue had him moving up to get more of it.

Lance was at an angle to Keen, and he reached down and fondled Keen's balls as he raised and lowered his head. In a really short time, Keen was jerking up and rising from the bed to bend over Lance as he shot long and hard. Lance pulled off just in time. Keen put his hand on Lance's wet hair and moved it over the thick mass. He took deep breaths and finally pulled Lance's face up to his and took his mouth, feeling like he wanted to go for hours now that the edge was off. He was still hard, and he wanted to take Lance's ass and make him moan and sigh and beg.

"Come up here and lie on your back for me. I'm gonna take you that way, so I can watch you while we fuck. I want to see your face, your eyes. I'll learn more about what you like that way. You okay with that?"

"Please...do it." Lance crawled up and did as he asked. Keen reached over to the bedside table and got the lube and the condoms. He turned back and when he saw the look of hunger on Lance's face he had to lean down and take another kiss. He tongue-fucked Lance's mouth and watched his eyes the whole time. The man spoke volumes with his eyes. He told Keen he loved how that felt, he loved what was happening, and he wanted more.

Keen was going to ask Lance to put his legs up over his shoulders, but instead Lance grabbed them and pulled them up and apart, presenting Keen with the whole package, cock, balls, and gaping, hungry hole. He took just a second to enjoy the sight. Lance was beautifully made. Keen intended to get into this position again soon and use his lips and tongue on every single inch of that view.

But now, now he had other things to do. He opened the condom and slid it on, then lubed it up. After that, he put some on his fingers and put two of them to the puckered hole waiting for him. He eased in his fingers, watching Lance's eyes the whole time. They closed for a second as he seemed to savour the first feeling of entry. Keen slid his fingers in further and began twisting them around, searching for that spot. Ah, there. Lance yelled and bucked up against his fingers.

Keen repeated the movement a couple more times then went back to moving his fingers in and out. He added another to them and looked to see how Lance took it. That was not a look of pain. He pushed carefully, nevertheless, until he was sure Lance was okay with it. He added a little more lube and then thrust them in and out, managing to rake across Lance's gland a few more times.

"Now, Keen, please. Oh God. That feels so good...so fuckin' good. I want to feel you in me. Want to see it." Lance was watching, his eyes going back and forth between Keen's eyes and what Keen did between his legs.

Keen pulled out his fingers and replaced them in one long lunge with his heavy dick. He sank in until he was flush against Lance's body. He took a second to feel the tightness and heat around him. Lance seemed tighter and hotter than anyone ever. Was that possible, or just because he wanted it to be true? He gave up thinking and started moving.

He put his hands on the backs of Lance's thighs since they were right in front of him and held on as he began to push in and pull out in a steadily increasing pace. He scooted up on his knees a little further so he could reach down and meet Lance's mouth. He stuck out his tongue and reached for Lance's as his hips kept up the rocking motion that had Lance moaning steadily.

Their tongues touched and slid against each other. Keen closed his mouth around Lance's tongue and sucked it hard into his mouth. He kept up the tight suction as his hips began to pound hard into the upturned ass. He wasn't sure how Lance breathed bent double like that but it sure did feel good. He took a second to ask, "You okay?"

"Never...better...never...more, come back..." and Keen was back into that mouth as requested. It would take him a really, really long time to get tired of this, this feeling...with this man. He was ready to ask Lance to move in and set up house and be his lover until they were both too old to get it up any more. Then he'd just kiss him for the rest of forever.

He pulled away a little and eased back so Lance had a better chance of breathing. He slowed his thrusts and leaned up to push in just so. He smiled as Lance jerked and gave just a little scream. Keen knew how he felt. Lance was so sensitive from being fucked long and hard and just a couple of touches to his gland like that...and that, and it was all over except for the shouting. Lance shot his load again, hard, cum reaching all the way up to his shoulders as he bucked and jerked, putting his arms up to pull Keen down to him as Keen started to jerk and with rhythmic pulses filled the condom with hot liquid.

Lance kept his arms around Keen and pulled him to him and just held him for a few minutes. He seemed to need to hold him, feel him close. Finally, he let Keen go and watched as he turned to ease off the condom and tie it, tossing it into the wastebasket near the table. There was a box of tissues on the table, and Lance reached for them. He grabbed some and cleaned Keen a little then himself. He threw them the way of the condom then eased himself into Keen's open arms.

"Is it just me…or was that…more…just more than usual?"

"Not just you. It was more…definitely more. I think I almost considered asking for your hand in marriage there for a second or two."

Lance laughed and held him tight, rolling with him until he was lying on top of Keen, looking down at him.

"Do I have to be the wife?"

"No, husband and husband. Equal. Goof. Besides, you can't be a wife. You can't cook."

"Oh, right. Well, it's off then. But can we still live in glorious sin and do this as often as possible?"

"Most definitely. Anything that good can not be a sin. Has to be a gift from God, you know? I know it's a popular belief…you know, just the opposite. But, I think that was about as powerful a statement as anything I've ever felt. It's a good thing. We're a good thing. How much time do we have before they come back and we have to be clean and presentable again?"

Lance looked over at the clock and sighed, "About half an hour."

"Not enough time at all. Let's hit the shower, and you behave now, you hear?"

"Me? You're the one with the wandering hands in there, you know?"

"Oh, that was me? Sorry." Keen tried to go for repentant.

"Don't be."

"I'm not, really." He laughed. "Come on. I've got to start the grill, and we've got to act like we haven't been fucking our brains out in here."

"That might take some powerful acting. I'm not going to be able to look at you without wanting you again, and it's gonna show."

"No duh. And if I kiss you like I want to right now, we'll have lips that will look bruised and swollen. One of these days, though, just you wait. We'll have time to do all kinds of things."

"Holding my breath, Keen. You are so...it."

Keen laughed and pulled him up and towards the shower. They only played a little and their lips did look well-used, but they were in the kitchen when Sandy and Kale returned with heavenly smelling brownies. There were a few awkward moments then things settled down.

Kale talked about life as a cop in Cincy, and Lance told some of his stories from Hawaii. Sandy related a few funny things that had happened in the ER and Keen even had a few from the gym. It was late when they all parted, agreeing to meet the next day for lunch downtown and to show Lance and Kale the gym and introduce Lance to the owner of the dojo.

As they said good night at the door, Kale asked Sandy if she was working the next night. When she said she wasn't, he asked her out to dinner and a movie. Her eyes lit up, and she agreed.

Keen hoped Kale really wanted to go out with her, and that he wasn't, again, giving him alone time with Lance. Keen knew she wanted to go out with Kale. Maybe something good would come of all this. Maybe he and Sandy would find what they'd been searching for, seemingly forever.

Chapter Five

The next day they met for lunch and planned their day. Keen and Lance were going to the gym then to meet the owner of the dojo. Lance was anxious to get started on his routines again. Sandy and Kale would go around and see some of what made Nashville the country music centre. They planned to meet for dinner at a nice restaurant Sandy liked then split again and go out on the town. Keen and Lance were going to a club where they could listen to music and dance together. Sandy and Kale were going to a movie then maybe to a club later.

"Are you guys okay with these plans? I mean, really? You don't have to go out just so we can spend time together. We can manage to see each other and get some time. I do have to admit, Sandy, that I'm really enjoying getting to know your brother," Keen said, trying not to gaze adoringly at Lance.

"Well, frankly, Keen, I have to admit the same thing. I'm enjoying getting to know yours, too. We aren't doing things just so you all can go suck face—I don't think so anyway. I'm having a good time with Kale."

Kale jumped in right on cue with, "Oh, hey. No problem, Kee. I like your sexy neighbour. Spending time with her is not a favour to you, believe me."

"Oooh, WTMI, dude," Lance said then laughed at Kale, when he cocked his head.

"Way Too Much Information." Keen supplied.

"Yeah, not sure I want to know how sexy you think my sister is," Lance supplied.

"Well, it's only fair. You think my brother's sexy," Kale returned.

"There is that. Gotta admit it. Sexy, hot, devastating is more like it."

"So, uh…are you coming home tonight, little brother?" Sandy asked, smiling smugly.

"Don't know. Do I have a curfew?" Lance laughed at her.

"Not at all. I'm just teasing you. You don't have to come home at all, long as I know where you are—especially if you're close, ya know?" Sandy teased.

"Yeah, he knows…and it's a definite possibility that after a few dances he might just be staying with me tonight. That okay?" Keen had definite plans for the evening, and he didn't want any misunderstandings later.

"That's fine. He's certainly old enough to make his own decisions and I don't have to worry that he's getting mixed up with the wrong kind of person now, do I?" Sandy quipped.

"Same goes. You two have a fun evening. Ka, when you come in, if my door's closed…walk on by."

"Maybe I won't come in," Kale shot back. Lance hooted, Sandy blushed, and Keen chuckled. Well, now. This could get real interesting.

* * * *

Lance was impressed with Keen's gym, and they played at working out on a few things. Keen got Lance a membership then they went to meet Hammer.

"Hammer?" Lance raised an eyebrow.

"Yep. He could hammer you right into the mat if he wanted to. You should see him do tai chi. He's the most graceful big man I've ever seen. You do that, too?"

"Yeah, I've trained in it. Not my favourite, but it has its place. I understand the concepts and agree with the positive effects it has, but I don't do as much of it. I'm partial to some of the other forms." He bounced a little on his toes "I could be borderline hyper. This really helps me. But I've had several classes, and I'd like to see him. Does he give classes personally, or does he have a staff?"

"Both, I think. I'm sure when he sees your skills he's gonna want to work with you. I'd like to see you work together. Do you show individually or in fights?"

"Mostly individual. I have done a few of the paired competitions. I don't like them as much. We'll see."

"Well, you sure put your skills to good use with Madman Manny."

"Yuck. Don't remind me. He was skanky. Tell me about this club we're going to. Are you really going to dance with me?"

"I hope so. It's crazy. There are all these rooms, and you can go dance however you feel at the moment. There's slow, romantic, buckle-polishing music in one and shake your booty in the other. There's usually a drag show if you want to go up and watch it. Sometimes there's a comedian, and they're usually pretty good. It's mostly a dance club with lots and lots of music. No back room, like Babylon, though." He figured Lance knew what he meant when he blushed and nodded.

"No problem. I'd rather take that home. Am I really staying at your house tonight?"

"You want to?"

"You know I do."

"Then, yeah."

"Cool."

* * * *

Lance and Hammer really hit it off. Keen was truly impressed when he saw them work together on a few things. Hammer was finding out how skilled Lance really was. Lance was getting used working with the big man. They put on quite a show.

"You lookin' for work?" Hammer said as they walked towards Keen.

"Um...I don't know. I'm visiting my sister. I just got in from Hawaii." Lance hadn't thought about working while he was here. Might be cool.

"Well, I have an opening, and I'd love to work with you. If you want to, come in and spend some time. I've got some guys who'd love to learn some of your moves, and they need a good teacher." He looked at Lance intently and continued. "I've got so many classes going, and these guys need that little extra. I think you're it. If you're interested, let me know."

"What do you think, Keen?"

"Me? I think you need to do whatever would make you happy. How long were you planning to stay? Will you be bored when both Sandy and I are working?"

That was something for Lance to think about. Weekends were great, but pretty soon, he'd be on his own.

"Looking for something to do? Make a little money? Sounds like a plan to me. Up to you, though. Those are just a few questions to ask yourself," Keen added.

"Hammer, can I get back to you? I'm interested. I need to think about things and see what I'm going to do. I promise I'll take the offer seriously and get back to you soon." It was obvious that Lance respected Hammer and would give the offer serious thought.

Lance and Keen left and were quiet as they walked towards Keen's gym. Keen knew Lance was spinning the offer around in his head and thinking about what to do.

"Can I help?" he offered, reaching over to touch Lance's hand in a quick gesture of support.

"You just did. I don't know what to think, ya know? I'd like to work with him. You were right. He's awesome. I'd learn a lot from him and enjoy working there. I could stay here for a while. I don't have to go back for a job, that's for sure. Maybe I could find something in computers here to back up the other job then make this my home." He wanted to see what Keen thought of him staying here.

"Would you be happy here, after Hawaii? It's very different. Ever seen snow?" Keen laughed at Lance's wide-eyed expression.

"There's an incentive. Cool."

"Why don't you take the job and plan to stay for six months or a year, and if you're not happy after that, move on to something else? But I have to tell you, I'm going to try very hard to make sure you're happy...so you'll stay.

Just fair warning." Keen loved the idea of Lance staying in Nashville, working down the street and…maybe, if things worked out between them…living with him…

"How are you going to make sure I'm happy?" Lance winked at him.

They'd gotten back to the gym and now walked towards Keen's office. Before Keen answered him, he pulled Lance into the office, locked the door and put his hand on Lance's chest, pushing him towards the big desk.

"I'm going to fuck you six ways to Sunday and love on you 'til you melt and ruin you for any other man." Keen liked the stunned look on Lance's face. "I'm going to take you out and wine and dine you and dance with you to slow, sweet songs, so we can hold each other and sway and rub against each other." He liked the heat in Lance's eyes. "I'm going to take you to great places and show you beautiful things that are just as wonderful as your home." He liked the smile on Lance's face. "I'm going to prove to you that you made the right decision in staying here to live and work and maybe love." He liked the happy look and the little gasp Lance made. "And I'm going to start right now."

Keen had watched scenes in movies where the guy raked his hand across a messy desk and laid his lover down on the bare wood. His desk was usually pretty clean so it wasn't quite the grand gesture. He did it anyway, and the look on Lance's face was enough to make him glad he did. After clearing a space, he took Lance's hand and pulled him around to the chair behind the desk. He sat and pulled Lance into his lap, facing him.

"You're crazy. We're going to tip over." Lance laughed and leant down to kiss him anyway.

Keen reached into his pocket for a condom and looked around for lubricant. Ah! Lotion. He turned and grabbed some from the shelf behind him. He set them both on the desk and turned back to look up at Lance.

"What do you think of my ideas for making sure you're happy?" he asked, reaching for the bottom of Lance's shirt and pulling it up and over his head.

"Mmmmmmph. Hey," he said, when he could see Keen again. "I like them...all of them. You looking for a roommate? I mean, when your brother's visit is over? I'd be close to Sandy, but the idea of being with you all the time...Oh, man."

"I think there's room. Let's keep the idea to ourselves right now. Let's be sure we're on the same page when Kale leaves then we'll revisit this plan." He knew he'd like it, but maybe Lance would get tired of him and want to go exploring.

"I won't change my mind."

"Go ahead and take the job if you want, and we'll see how things go. Sound good?" He worked on the snap and zipper of Lance's jeans now, smiling when Lance reached down to help him and their hands got tangled in their haste.

"Sounds good. No one will come in, right?"

Keen smiled at his worry. "I'd never take a chance on embarrassing you. You're not for show. You're mine only."

"Yep. Yours only. I like the sound of that." Lance smiled wickedly at Keen. "I've seen some of your athletic moves. Wanna show me some of your executive moves? Nice desk, by the way." Lance stood and shucked his jeans and shorts, taking his shoes with them.

"Executive moves, huh? Like this?" Keen took Lance by the shoulders and guided him to the desk, laying him back over it. During the next hour he would use both athletic and executive moves.

Ever mindful of Lance's comfort, Keen drew his shirt over his head and, pulling Lance up for a moment, put it under his back so his skin wouldn't drag on the desktop. Lance watched him closely but let him do whatever he wanted, moving as directed. Keen had Lance's pants down to his feet in no time and was bent over the hard cock that seemed to reach up for him. Reaching down, he pulled Lance's pants off one foot, while sliding his tongue up Lance's cock. Lance gasped and brought his legs up and wrapped them around Keen's waist.

"Well, hey there," Lance said, arms reaching up to pull Keen up to him. Keen resisted at first, taking time to remove his own slacks and shorts. Moving closer to Lance, he smiled down at Lance, with sex in his eyes.

"Hey, yourself," Keen answered, bending the last little bit needed to put their lips together at the same time their cocks met and mashed against each other. Both of them moaned at the twin contacts. Keen kissed Lance while reaching between them to grasp both cocks in his hand and pressed them harder together. While Lance whined into his mouth, Keen moved his hand up and down as much as he could with them that close together.

Keen pulled away from Lance's mouth to rise up and pay attention to what he was doing with his hand. With his other, he reached down to and teased Lance's right nipple. At Lance's gasp, Keen went a little further, pinching the tight bud. Receiving another groan and jerk, he moved over to the left one. Never stopping the motion of the hand working both their cocks, Keen winked down at Lance. Lance smiled up at Keen and put one of his hands on Keen's in both areas, helping to both jerk them off and tweak his own nipple.

A few seconds later, they were both trying to muffle shouts as they came together, bathing their hands and Lance's stomach with cum. Breathing heavily, Keen leaned to take a quick kiss from Lance then stood and reached for Lance's hands to pull him up to sit on the edge of the desk.

"That was better than anything I've ever done at this desk before, I can tell you that," Keen said.

"I think I'm glad to hear that," Lance answered. "Uh, tissues, several of them?"

"I think a washcloth and a towel would be better. Just a second." Keen let go of Lance and moved to a door Lance hadn't noticed. Ah, the executive washroom. Keen came in and cleaned them both, taking kisses and nibbles of Lance's neck in between swipes of the cloth. Lance took that from him and finished up. Setting them aside, Lance reached for Keen and pressed in for another kiss, this one longer and deeper than before.

In a surprise move, Lance took hold of Keen's shoulders and turned him so that Keen was sitting on the desk. Keen, too, spent a little time spread out on that shiny surface while Lance worked hard between his legs. Keen knew he'd never look at his desk the same way again.

* * * *

Keen and Lance left the gym, both smiling and relaxed as they walked back to Keen's big Suburban and talked about plans for the evening. Admittedly, neither was paying much attention to their surroundings.

They both snapped to when they heard a cry from right behind them and someone bumped hard into Keen then took off running. They turned to find an elderly lady on the street, holding her arm and trying to get up.

"He...he...took my purse. He hit me and knocked me down." Her eyes were huge when she realised she'd actually been attacked. "He took my purse." She was shaking and alarmingly pale. She was a tiny thing, with beautiful white hair.

Lance and Keen looked at each other and, in a heartbeat, without words, came to a decision. Keen went to the lady, and Lance took off after the punk with the purse.

Lance was fast. He dodged and weaved in between people on the street. It was only a couple of minutes before he had the guy in sight. He sprinted faster and overtook him. He reached out for the purse, snagged it and held on, dragging the young punk to a stop. Next thing Lance knew, the guy pulled a knife and took a swipe at him.

He managed to pull back and avoid the knife. Taking another step back, he swung his left leg up and hit the boy on the arm holding the purse. The bag dropped to the ground, and he howled. He turned to run away, and Lance bent a little and swept his right leg across, knocking the thief's legs right out from under him. He went down hard with another howl.

"Good job, again." Keen said from behind Lance's shoulder as he straightened. Keen reached down, taking the boy by the shoulders, pulling him up. Lance retrieved the purse, and they faced each other.

"We've got to stop meeting like this," Keen couldn't help saying.

Lance laughed and said, "What about the old lady?"

"Hey, watch it, young 'un," he heard from behind Keen. There stood the spunky little lady whose purse had been stolen, holding her arm close to her side.

"Sorry, ma'am. Here's your purse. Are you okay?"

"Little fart broke my arm."

Lance couldn't hold in his quick snort of laughter. She was a hoot.

"I've called the police, and they're on the way, as well as an ambulance for Phoebe here." He nodded as Phoebe started to sputter. "I know you don't need no danged ambulance, but it's too late. They'll just take you in and set your arm, I bet. Don't worry about it."

"I'll look like some invalid being carted off in that thing. They better not turn on the sirens! And no lights, either. And I'm sittin' up, not layin' down."

She was pretty sure about how things were going to go, and soon, if the sound of sirens was any clue.

The guy in Keen's hold tried to get away, jerking against Keen's grip. Not happening. Keen held tight and gave him a look. He stilled.

"Don't you let that snake go, hear me?" Her voice was sharp.

"I'm not, hon. Don't you worry. We'll see he's taken in," Keen assured her.

"Aw, come on, she's got her bag back. Let go, can't ya?" the punk begged.

"Too late. Ya should've thought of that before you knocked down a helpless old lady and stole from her," Phoebe said.

"Helpless, hell," the thief muttered, sighing as police and ambulance pulled up at the same time. There was a crowd gathered now, plenty of witnesses.

One of the officers, Ragan again, looked at Keen and Lance and said, "Didn't I see you at the station this morning?"

"Yes, sir. We were giving a report on what happened at the airport."

"You all get around, don't you? What went on here?" the other officer asked.

They explained quickly, with a few people chiming in about Lance's quick feet and his bravery against the guy with the knife.

The paramedics got Phoebe settled, according to her specific requests. Keen and Lance both smiled as they heard her telling them how she would travel or they could just leave her alone. They went over to find out where she was going to be taken.

She told Lance to get a piece of paper and a pen from her purse then had him write down her phone number and her address. She wanted them to come see her tomorrow or the next day. They promised they would.

After the ambulance left, they finished telling the story to the policemen and finally headed back to the truck. They were full of adrenaline now that it was over. It hadn't been nearly as bad as the mess yesterday at the airport, but for a minute, it had been a little hairy.

"What now?" Lance asked, climbing in and buckling up. He glanced over at Keen and they burst out laughing.

"We can't seem to stay out of trouble. We're gonna get a name at the station. Maybe we ought to get deputised or something, huh?"

"Yeah. Chaos magnets, that's us. What about Phoebe, wasn't she cute? Are we gonna go see her tomorrow?"

"Sure, I'd like to. You?" Keen didn't know if Lance would be into visiting the older lady.

"Absolutely. Take her some flowers or something. She was something else. Feisty little thing, wasn't she?" Lance laughed and nodded when Keen agreed she was a real character.

Keen checked his watch and looked over at Lance.

"I'm pretty hyped up. Not ready to go home yet. Let's go walk around downtown. We'll hit a couple of shops, get some goodies and take them home. Sandy'll love it. I know what she likes. I'm thinking it wouldn't hurt to stay in her good graces. We'll surprise her. There's a place that has 'divine pastries'. Her words, not mine. Okay with you?"

"Yeah, man. Anything. I'm kinda pumped, too. Need to walk it off. I'd love to get something for Sandy. Maybe we could get some for Phoebe, too." Lance had evidently really liked her. He smiled, just talking about her. "She'd probably be tickled. I'm ready for some walking and shopping. Boy, does that sound gay!"

"Aw well, after the last few minutes, you don't have to worry about your macho image. You can kick ass with the best of them."

"Does seem to have come in handy lately, huh? Want me to teach you some moves? After all, you taught me some of your executive ones..." They broke into laughter at that. They both had some pretty good moves.

Keen luckily found a place to park and the two walked all over downtown Nashville. They found the shop Sandy liked and purchased some of her favourites. After much deliberation, Keen suggested they get Phoebe a small cake and, having noticed that her outfit and her purse were both pink, had her name written on it in pretty pink icing.

Keen and Lance got home before Kale and Sandy so they took their goodies in and set them in the kitchen with labels for 'Sandy', 'Phoebe', and 'Anyone'. They were in the workout room when they heard the door open.

"Hey, honeys, I'm home," Kale yelled.

"Cute, Ka."

Kale walked in and Keen punched his arm.

"How was your afternoon?"

"Fun. Sandy's cool. We saw lots of great places. She took me to the Ryman Auditorium and the Country Music Hall of Fame. That was really interesting. We drove by the Parthenon and the Capitol building and then she parked downtown and we checked out Second Street and Broadway. Saw the Spaghetti Factory. I wanna go there to eat, man. Saw the stadium, too. Walked our feet off. She's promised to take me to the Blue Bird Café and some cool bookstore, too. I'm ready for a shower then food." They'd been heading back towards the kitchen. When they got there, Kale's eyes lit up.

"Oooh, sugary food. Gimme."

"You always were a sucker for sweets."

"Me? You seem to have bought out the store. Who's Phoebe?" By then Lance had ambled in and joined them. They related their afternoon adventures.

"No fuckin' way," was Kale's response. He shook his head. "Kee, you all are not safe out together. You seem to draw trouble to you."

"Told ya," Lance said, nodding. "Chaos magnets."

"Wait 'til Sandy hears about baby brother's adventures today. She'll want to lock you up."

"Why? We handled everything fine. Do ya think we could downplay things a bit? There's no sense in freaking her out. Besides, I'm not the kid she thought I was, remember?" Lance didn't want Sandy upset, but he wasn't going to be limited either.

"Dude, I was teasing. She'll be fine with it. She's cool. We had a really good day," Kale told him.

They went their separate ways to clean up before going to the restaurant where all of them would share supper.

* * * *

The meal was delicious, filled with banter and laughter and hot looks between two sets of partners for the evening. Kale and Sandy really were having a great time together, and there was no doubt about Lance and Keen. The respective afternoons were discussed and Keen and Lance told them about Phoebe and what a hoot she was. Keen told her that he and Lance were going to visit her tomorrow and check on her. That's when Keen told Sandy about the treats he'd bought for her. She was duly appreciative, promising to share with Kale.

They parted ways, Kale and Sandy heading out to a comedy club and maybe on to dance later. Lance and Keen were going to a bar that was one of Keen's favourite places.

The bar was for couples and not one of the places to pick up someone for the night. It was for people who wanted to be with each other and dance and maybe drink a little and not be hit on or hassled. Keen'd almost felt embarrassed before because he didn't fit in. Tonight he felt like he was one of those people the club was made for. He was excited about taking Lance there.

The kid cleaned up nice—and Keen really had to stop thinking of him as a kid. He was only five years younger. It wasn't as if keen was robbing the cradle, for heaven's sake. Lance was old enough to know who and what he was and frankly, who and what he wanted.

Keen looked over at Lance as they drove to the club. "Did I tell you that you look really nice?"

"Nah, but thanks. You, too. You're one of those people who wear clothes well. Good body, and you always look like you're comfortable. I just throw stuff on and hope it goes okay."

"You do fine, but thanks. Ah, here's our exit. I hope you like this place. It's not as wild as some we could go to, and if you're not comfortable here, we'll try another place. I just want to dance with you. Hold you and nibble on your neck a little."

"Oh, now. I'm thinking the place doesn't matter if that's what you have in store for me. Bring it on." Lance sounded eager to get in and get on the dance floor. He evidently had some holding of his own he wanted to do.

Lance was nearly bouncing as they stepped around the crowd by the door of Men's Limited and headed inside. As they did, Keen saw a couple leaning against the wall by the door in a heated clinch. Just as he passed, he heard "Want you" answered by "Mm-hmm." He caught the smile on Lance's face. He'd heard it, too.

Keen took Lance's hand, and his heart jumped a little as Lance glanced over at him.

"I love the idea of being able to do this without fear. This is nice," Lance said, squeezing his hand. "I was never in a position to show affection before. It was such a taboo at work, never talked about or accepted. And I really didn't go to bars with dates. I've been to some, but never with someone special, like tonight."

Keen gave Lance a hot look and a hand squeeze for that then he led Lance from room to room, giving him a feel for the place. They watched a little of the drag show and laughed at how campy it was. When they passed a big room, Lance hesitated. Keen watched him as he took in the room. It was darkened and had a ramped up mirror ball. There were interesting shards of light in strange shapes thrown around the room, but slowly, so it enhanced the mood.

"Can we...?" Lance began.

"Definitely in the plan," Keen finished, tugging his hand and pulling him closer. That was where the holding and nibbling would happen.

They ended in the main bar, a very large space, lit in the serving area and not so much in the rest of the room. They caught a table along the wall with a good view of the dance floor and ordered from the good-looking waiter who came by. They placed their chairs together, their shoulders and legs pressed tight as they watched the more upbeat dancing.

Lance asked Keen how he found this bar. "I come here with a couple of friends once in a while, usually feeling like a third wheel. Sometimes I bring Sandy."

"No way." Lance was shocked.

"Honey, not everyone in here is gay."

"But...?" The look on Lance's face was priceless. He looked around like he might be able to spot obvious imposters. Keen thought it was funny.

"Yeah, it's a gay bar. But some people come to gawk, to see something they can go back and talk about. Others come with friends of theirs who are gay, like Sandy does. There are lots of different reasons."

"And you?"

Keen thought about it for a minute before he answered truthfully, "Acceptance, camaraderie, fun, friends, dancing, drinks, and laughter. It's a place where I can hold your hand or lean across and give you a kiss. Where I can dance close with you and steal kisses or nibbles and know it's okay."

"Sounds like a little piece of heaven to me," Lance agreed.

As soon as they finished their drinks, Lance looked at Keen and he nodded, pulling him up.

As they headed into the darkened room they saw the couple from outside. They followed them right onto the dance floor, and Keen took Lance into his arms. Lance's face went straight to Keen's shoulder, and they began to dance. They started slowly, getting a feel for how well the other moved. Both were pleasantly surprised.

"You're good," Keen whispered.

"So're you. This is so neat. I like it in here." Lance was so obviously pleased that he could cuddle and dance, really dance, here. He snuggled closer.

"My step-mother, Nancy, made me take dance and gymnastics early on when I got interested in the martial arts. She said it would help and some day I'd be glad. She was right about both. You?" Lance asked.

"I've always liked to dance. Sandy and I come in here some and dance, but with her I don't do this," and, with those words, he leant down and took Lance's lips. They kept dancing around the room, moving rhythmically to the music, gliding, and turning. They eased out of the kiss, not taking it any further. Lance put his head back to Keen's shoulder and got a squeeze from him.

They danced through song after song, not knowing or caring what the words were. They were lost in the joy of holding, with the occasional sweet kiss or secret touch that sent pulses racing. It was dark and warm and they built up a slow passion that drew them closer and closer as time passed.

About an hour and a half later, Lance looked at Keen and he nodded. They turned, as one, and left the dance floor and the club. It was comfortably quiet on the way home.

When they arrived, Keen walked in and yelled for Kale. Getting no answer, he checked his room and found that they were alone. As one, they turned towards Keen's room.

As they neared the door, Lance said, "You gonna take me to bed?"

Keen laughed and grabbed him, pulling him into the room. "That was definitely in the plan. Shower first. Hot and sweaty here." They headed to the bathroom together, and Keen stopped in the doorway to take Lance into his arms. Lance looked up at him.

"I really enjoyed tonight. The dancing was great, and I see what you mean about the club. I'd love to go back again." Lance hummed one of the songs they'd danced to close to the end of the evening.

"We will. I loved dancing with you. You feel really good in my arms." Keen tightened them around Lance now and danced him on into the bathroom.

"That's true. I do feel good in your arms. Wanna keep me there?" Lance teased back.

"Can't. Gotta get the shower going. Really want to get naked with you now." Keen almost laughed at the eager look on Lance's face.

"Okay, then." Lance started to remove his clothes, but Keen stepped up and took his hand, placing it on his shirt buttons. He reached for Lance's. A quick study, Lance began to undress Keen while he did the same for him. The process got slower and their bodies got closer as they progressed.

Soon the shower was running, and they stepped in together. They weren't in a hurry tonight. They took time to caress and explore as the water pelted them with heat and silkiness. They enjoyed the textures of skin and hair, the smells of the soaps and each other. They especially went for the tastes of skin and water combined, as well as the heat and flavour of their mouths as their passion escalated. They rinsed, dried, and headed for the bed.

Lance stood by the bed, waiting for his lover while Keen turned off the overhead light and tilted the shade on the dresser's lamp, making the room more conducive to romance.

"That's nice," Lance commented on Keen's efforts as he also put on some soft jazz, very low in the background.

"I'm trying to make this memorable for you." Keen admitted.

"Mission accomplished," Lance opened his arms for Keen, putting an end to the mood setting. Keen walked right into them and their mouths met in the most aggressive kiss of the night. Tongues clashed as they met and twirled together in an attempt to gather in more flavours. Keen crushed Lance's lips under his, and they both moaned a little as they tightened their arms and pressed together, head to toe. Their cocks strained forward as they rubbed against each other. The friction had them both leaking and hard.

They seemed to be doing things simultaneously tonight. Keen reached down to take Lance in hand at the same time as Lance reached for him. Together they tugged and sighed.

"Feels so good," Lance muttered.

"Mm-hmm, harder," Keen replied and groaned when Lance complied.

"I'm gonna lose it pretty quickly if we don't stop this. I've wanted you all night." Lance seemed to think he had to apologise for being so far along.

"Not alone there, and so what? We need to take the edge off a little, anyway. I want to spend a really long time with you, long, slow, and sexy. That's what I want tonight. So, I think maybe..." He slid right down Lance's body and took his heavy dick in his mouth. Keen wanted to taste him so bad. He hadn't managed more than a couple of strong licks along the length of it, before Lance shot.

"Uh...how would you feel about getting tested...together...tomorrow? I'd love to...if you...I mean, if you think you want to be exclusive, we could..." Keen trailed off. He couldn't believe he was stuttering and stammering as if he was unsure of himself. He wasn't. He was just unsure of Lance.

"You mean it? I could so do that. I do want to be exclusive. I don't have this great need for scouting out anyone else." He looked down at Keen as if he was everything in the world he wanted. "I want to be with you. The idea of being able to do it all without the latex, man, that just rocks."

"Yeah, same here." Keen said, looking up at Lance.

"You are so special. I've never been with anyone I wanted to be that close to, ya know?" Lance's eyes lit up and he smiled.

"Again, I feel the same."

"Okay, tomorrow, you and me. Health department. Then, soon, just us. Come 'ere, you." He pulled up on Keen's shoulders.

Keen went, knowing what Lance had in mind. He was good at it, too. Before long, no more edges. They finally eased down onto the bed and settled against each other. Keen had condoms under the pillow, along with the lube. He wanted Lance to make love to him tonight.

"Hey." Keen got Lance's attention away from his chest, where he was drawing a line from one of his nipples to the other with his tongue. Lance looked up, questioningly.

"Hey?"

"I want you inside me…okay?" Keen wasn't afraid of asking for what he wanted, but he wanted to be sure Lance was up for that.

"Absolutely. I've thought about it. You are the sexiest, most gorgeous man and I want you. Can I just take over for a while?"

"Certainly. Do anything you want. Search and explore, but promise you'll end up deep inside me."

"Maybe I'll find some of your sensitive spots along the way, hmm? Don't worry. I won't forget what my goal is. I'm so ready for you." Lance took Keen's hand and brought it to his hard cock and sucked in a deep breath as Keen used his hand expertly. He didn't want Lance to lose it yet, though. He eased back.

"I want you on your hands and knees, if that's okay with you," Lance said.

"You're the boss, remember? Don't be shy. Order me around. Take me however you want. If I don't want to do something, I won't, but we're equal here. Thinking of you as a kid is something I've given up, okay? You're plenty man enough for me and for this." Keen liked the idea of them being equal here in the bedroom. He was a little older and had his life all set up, but Lance wasn't far behind.

Lance crawled right up him and took Keen's lips in a crushing kiss. His tongue thrust inside Keen's mouth and took inventory. He met Keen's tongue and they pushed against each other and moved back into Lance's mouth. He sucked on Keen's tongue and felt him shudder. Ah! He'd found something that made Keen shake. He decided to find more.

Lance ended the kiss and went on to map the whole of Keen's upper body. He paid close attention to his neck and chest. Keen's nipples were sensitive, and Lance spent time making them hard little peaks. He licked then blew on them. Sucking hard, Lance had Keen arching on the bed as he groaned and grabbed Lance's head, holding it tight to him, wanting more.

"I love it," Lance sighed against Keen's stomach, pausing to lick his navel and smiling as Keen sucked in, his stomach muscles showing.

"Mmm, what?" Keen seemed to be floating and unsure of what he'd heard. "You what?" He raised his head from the pillow and looked down into Lance's eyes.

"I love finding things that make you respond like that. I'm keeping a list in my head."

"Clever man. I like that. I'll do the same, but...oh!" Keen jerked and his shoulders came up off the bed a bit as Lance touched his tongue to the very tip of Keen's dick and pressed in. At that response, he went back again.

He took Keen in his hand and made a very careful study of his cock. He looked closely and licked here and there, noting how Keen liked this or that. Enjoying himself greatly, he took the head into his mouth and sucked gently, licking the tip at the same time. Ah...okay. He took more in, as much as he could and sucked as hard as he could, and Keen yelled. Using his other hand, he teased Keen's balls gently as he continued his lesson in Keen's Cock 101. To pass, he had to get him off. Lance went back to work and before long he had aced the class.

He watched avidly as Keen shot great wads of cum amid grateful groans and shudders. Lance smoothed the creamy stuff over Keen's stomach and smiled up into his eyes.

"No more edges for you."

"Not one." Keen smiled back at him and reached down to caress his hair. He reached up and took the lube and a condom and passed them to Lance. Eagerly, Keen sat up and pressed a quick kiss to Lance's lips before turning and rising up on his hands and knees for him.

"I want to feel you pushing into me hard and deep. It's been a while, and I've thought about it a lot since meeting you."

"God, you are so sexy. Just look at you," Lance was entranced with the sight and the thought that Keen wanted him to take him like that. He covered himself and slicked his fingers and took care of smoothing some around Keen's eager hole. When he eased his fingers in, he couldn't help the smile when Keen shivered and moaned.

Keen's voice was a little quivery as he tried to make his wishes known. "I don't want to sound bossy or slutty, but could you maybe hurry?"

Lance was quick to meet his needs, making short work of stretching Keen enough to take him without pain. Replacing his fingers with his hard cock, he eased into his lover. Keen let out a gratified groan and pushed back until Lance was seated all the way to the hilt. Lance thrust hard for good measure and Keen moaned again.

Lance gave himself free rein and thrust into Keen over and over. He didn't even try for angles and turns and varying speed. He just fucked him like he obviously wanted to be fucked. He moved his hand over Keen's back, pressing in, scratching, and rubbing as he continued his forceful thrusts.

"Yes, God, Lance. What I needed..." Keen's voice rasped and shook.

"What I wanted to give you, what you need," Lance said, on a pull out. "So you'll want to keep me around," he finished on a return thrust.

Keen snorted and pushed back again. "Fuck me, Lance, just a little more and I'm done for. God, you feel good in me...so good." Keen's voice trailed off, and he just accepted the faster, harder thrusts that followed. Lance reached down and took Keen's cock in his hand and squeezed once, and Keen shot so hard Lance thought Keen would pass out. Keen dropped to the bed so fast that Lance landed on him.

"Oomph," Keen laughed. He turned his head to look back at Lance. "Don't stop. Please..."

Lance spread Keen's legs a little so he could continue his thrusts. He was ready to shoot, and in this new position, he could love on Keen a little. He ran his tongue up Keen's back and nibbled on his shoulder blade on his way to his neck. Just as he lunged hard and started to come, he sucked up a livid mark on Keen's neck. He eased out and took care of the condom before returning to Keen's open arms.

"It might sound corny, but thank you so much. I didn't know how much I had been missing it. I guess it's been a while," Keen said, taking Lance into his arms and settling him against him comfortably.

"Glad I could help out." Lance sounded short, a little like he was hurt. What had he said? Oh.

"Lance, hey, look at me. Can I rephrase that? That sounded like you were just a pick up that had done me a favour." When he saw Lance's eyes, he knew he'd hit it on the head. "Come on, you know better. After the night we had you know it's more than that." Keen reached to turn Lance's face to his, looking into his eyes as he said, "You were great, you made me feel wonderful. It was more…just more, because it was you."

"I'm sorry. I sounded silly, huh? I know. You're right. Put it down to performance anxiety." Lance laughed at himself.

"Put your fears to rest. That was…better than great. I thought I was gonna pass out."

"Really?" Lance was obviously tickled.

"Yeah. I've thought about you doing that, a lot. You're very special to me. With you, it's not just sex. It's more."

Lance blushed, and Keen leaned to kiss him. It was soft and sweet. He proceeded to show Lance just how special he was.

Before long, Lance was so sensitised after Keen kissed, licked, nibbled, and tasted every millimetre of his body that he shook from head to toe. He moved to do the same to Keen and seemed to enjoy the exercise. Keen had a beautiful body that Lance became wonderfully familiar with it. He, like Keen, left no place untouched. As he came back up to Keen's head, he placed his head into Keen's neck and breathed deep.

"Wanna just nap a while with me? I'm feeling pretty mushy right now," Keen asked, and Lance nodded against him. They settled in together and were soon asleep in each other's arms.

Keen woke twice during the night, reaching for Lance. The first time, Keen fell upon him like he was starving. He kissed Lance voraciously and pressed hard against him. They were becoming so attuned to each other's needs, Lance merely lined up their cocks and rocked until they both came hard, spraying against their stomachs.

The second time they woke, they just smiled at each other, tightened their arms and kissed until they slept again. Keen thought he probably smiled in his sleep all night. He knew he held Lance to him, turning with him, sliding against him, absently stroking him as he settled back to sleep each time.

Chapter Six

They woke to the phone ringing by Keen's bed. He slid out from under Lance's arm to reach for it and caught it on the third ring.

"Is it okay to come over? You all wanna share breakfast?" It was Sandy, and she sounded barely awake.

"Sure. Uh...is Kale still there? Did you all...I mean...?" He couldn't ask if they'd made love with her brother listening in.

"Oh my God, did we! He's as good as I've always imagined you to be. I am..." Suddenly the phone went silent, and he wondered if she'd hung up.

Then Kale came on and said, "Mind your own business, Kee."

Keen laughed and told his brother, "I'm so happy for you all. Really. She's the best friend I've got and—"

"Stay out of it. You wanna do breakfast or not?" Kale didn't sound mad, just not into sharing. Keen was okay with that. They'd talk later. Hell, Sandy could have grilled him about Lance. Of course, she knew what they'd been up to.

"Yeah, sorry. Let's meet in about half an hour. Over here's fine. I've got good breakfast stuff. Tell her she has to make the blueberry muffins to get in the door." He hung up as he heard Kale repeating his message. He turned to find Lance watching him.

"Hey. Good morning." He leant over to take a kiss.

Lance gave it eagerly and moaned as it deepened. He twisted more fully, and they spent a few minutes kissing and nuzzling and waking up.

"I take it my sister and your brother had a good night, too." Lance smiled, obviously thinking about that. "All in the family has a whole new meaning."

"Yeah, I gather, but Kale isn't into sharing. I won't hassle them about it. I do think it's cool, though. You okay with it?"

"Hell, yeah. Wouldn't it be great if..." He never finished the question.

"Hold that thought. We've got them coming over in a few minutes. We need to shower and get into the kitchen and start coffee and other breakfasty things." He rolled out and reached to pull the cover from a yawning Lance. He grinned as he watched Lance scratching his chest and stomach. Lance looked up and saw Keen watching then blushed.

Keen reached to pull him out of bed, saying, "We're gonna go see Phoebe this morning. That should be cool. I want to see how she's set up, if she can handle things okay with her arm in a cast."

Lance stood and followed Keen to the bathroom then leaned on the counter as Keen got the shower going. "You care about people a lot. I've noticed that about you. You don't just blow them off, even strangers. You take time for them. Don't blush. I think it's great. I'm well past infatuated, you know." Suddenly, it seemed, Lance was talking about more than just being impressed with Keen's character.

Keen turned back to reach for him and pulled him into a tight embrace. He wasn't all that comfortable talking about himself or hearing about himself in such glowing terms.

"Thank you, for the compliment and the sentiment. Both are welcome. I wish I had time to explore them a little further, and don't think I'm forgetting the last part. I just want to have time to respond. And I don't. Come on, sexy, let's clean up and go greet our siblings." He laughed at the way that sounded.

Keen was really looking forward to today, spending time with Sandy and Kale then visiting Phoebe and learning more about her. It all took on more meaning with Lance joining him. He, too, had passed the infatuation stage rather quickly. A chuckle escaped him as Lance dragged him into the spray.

Breakfast was great fun once the first period of awkwardness was broken after they all burst out laughing at about the same time. They all ate heartily and discussed their plans for the day.

Keen said, "Lance and I are going to see Phoebe. We want to see how she's doing this morning."

Kale said, "Well, we're going to laze around the house and we'll be responsible for supper." This got a laugh and a pink face from Sandy, causing Keen to wonder what could be so funny about planning supper.

Lance grabbed the cake they'd gotten for Phoebe, and they headed out. Keen drove to her address. The closer he got, the more worried he became. This wasn't a safe part of town. Lance was looking around with the same kind of expression. Surely Phoebe didn't live here. He finally found the right building, and he and Lance shared a look.

"Can't be. This place seriously sucks, Keen. Come on, let's go see if we can find her."

They were parked in front of a rundown apartment house that had seen better days twenty years ago. It should have been condemned. There was graffiti on the walls, none of it what one would call art. Some of the words made Keen cringe, thinking that the sweet little lady they met yesterday lived here and walked past that every day.

They went up the broken steps and into the front door, wondering what they'd find inside. It was dark just inside the door, and it was broad daylight outside. The light was broken and there was very little light coming in through the door. They could see a hallway going back on the left and stairs on the right. Her address indicated she lived on the second floor so they started up. Keen was feeling more and more concerned about Phoebe's living conditions.

They found her number on a door on the left of the hallway about half way down. Keen knocked and waited. They heard nothing.

"Phoebe, it's Keen and Lance. We helped you yesterday. We've come to see how you're doing." He wanted her to know who was knocking. He hoped she didn't open her door here very often. "Are you in there? Are you okay?"

They heard an "Oh!" from inside and some shuffling then a chain being removed, followed by three or four locks clicking open. The door opened a crack, and Phoebe peeked out at them. She opened the door wide and a huge smile lit her wrinkled face.

"Oh, my boys!" Delight rang in her voice as she stood and looked at them as if she couldn't believe they were there.

"Hello, Miss Phoebe," Lance said, smiling down at her. "We've come to bring you a little treat and to see how you're doing with the cast." He leant down and kissed her cheek.

Her eyes filled with tears, and she couldn't seem to say anything.

"May we come in?" Keen asked, edging in the doorway.

"Oh, forgive me. Of course, come in. What have you brought me?" Her smile was like a child on Christmas. "I can't believe you came to see me. No one comes to see me." Her one arm was in the cast and the other was up to her neck in a gesture of surprise.

"We shopped yesterday for my sister at her favourite bakery and decided to get you a little something. You can eat cake, can't you?" What if she wasn't allowed to have it for some reason, he thought, maybe they…

"Oh, yes indeed. What kind is it? Oh, it doesn't matter. I haven't had cake in so long…" Her watery eyes were happy, like a little kid's.

"Can I take this to your kitchen?" Lance offered. "Maybe you'd like a piece now. I'll cut one for you." He sounded eager to be doing something nice for the sweet woman.

Keen knew how he felt.

"Here, come sit down with me while Lance gets you some cake," Keen said, leading her over to a shabby little loveseat. He wanted to ask her some questions about her situation. He didn't know why he felt responsible for her, but he did. Yesterday, she'd seemed like a spitfire, ready to take on the world. Today, she seemed smaller, needier, more lonely. He hated the way it made him feel.

"Would you boys like some cake, too?" she asked as she eased down onto the seat with Keen.

"No, ma'am. We just had a really big breakfast," Keen answered.

"Oh, well, maybe I shouldn't..." She looked upset, worried that she shouldn't eat in front of them. It was obvious, though, that she couldn't wait for some cake.

"No, you go ahead. Do you mind if I ask you a few questions?" Keen asked, looking through to the small kitchen at Lance putting the cake on a plate for Phoebe. Lance looked up and caught his eye and shook his head, sadly.

"Sure, what do you want to know?" Phoebe settled back and looked at Keen.

"How long have you lived here? Aren't you scared?" Once he started, he couldn't stop. "Are you safe here? Are you alone? Do you need anything?"

"Well, I guess I've lived here for about five years...yes, Ally died about five years ago, and when it was all over, there wasn't enough for me to keep the house we'd shared for over sixty-five years. Ally was...she was..." She paused and looked at him and at Lance who was coming into the room with the cake. She made a decision.

"She was the love of my life. We lived together in a lovely little house, and she taught and I wrote. We were supremely happy, Ally and I. She died of cancer and the bills took everything. This is all I can afford. I know it's not much, but..."

"Honey, we're not knocking it. We're just worried about you." Keen said.

"But...why would you? You don't know me." She seemed truly bewildered by the kindness of these two men.

"You said you wrote? Would I have read anything you've written? Were you published?" Keen asked, changing the subject.

Phoebe clearly tried not to inhale the cake all at once, pausing a couple of times, but she made short work of it. Lance just got up from the floor where he'd dropped, took her plate, got her another piece and brought it back without a word spoken. She started in on it.

"Oh, I'm sorry. You asked me something. Mmm…this is so good. Thank you all so much." She devoured the second piece then handed her plate to Lance when he stood up and shook her head, indicating she didn't want more now.

Lance looked for something for her to drink, but found nothing. He got her a glass of water and took it to her. She took it gratefully and drank deeply.

"Writing. Yes. I was published, but I don't know if you would have read anything I wrote. It was pretty specialised. As you may have guessed, Ally and I were lesbians — before it was cool to be so." She smiled a little at her joke. "We thumbed our noses at our families, at society, made a life for ourselves, and never regretted a day." She looked from one to the other and asked, "Does that make you want to leave? Are you sorry you came to see me now?"

Keen was quick to relieve her mind. He smiled at her, feeling compassion and, now, a sort of kinship. "Phoebe, hon, we're gay. I've only known Lance a very few days, but we are well on our way to being a couple." He looked at Lance, and they smiled at each other, too. "The only thing that bothers me about your story is how you lost her. I'm so sorry." He reached out to pat her on the hand.

"Thank you, dear," she said, covering his hand with hers.

"Tell me about your writing, please. I'd love to know more about you." Lance took over with the request.

"You two can't possibly be interested in a ninety-year-old woman. You have so much you could be doing."

"Please, ma'am. I really do want to know more. What did you write?" Lance asked again.

Keen was surprised when she attempted to get up. He jumped up to help her, and she led them both over to an old desk. On it was a stack of books, all by T. R. Tremaine. Wait a minute. Keen looked at her and back to the stack. No way. He'd read every book of Tremaine's. He couldn't believe she had, too. They were so...well...they were erotic literature, gay erotic literature. He tried not to blush as he turned to her, and she smiled at him in delight.

"I've read every book Tremaine ever wrote. I'm thrilled you like him, too," He said

"Would you like me to autograph yours for you?" She waited for it to hit him. It didn't take long.

"No way." His eyes popped wide open. "Oh my God! Phoebe! You're T.R. Tremaine?" He was stunned. These books were famous in the gay world. Well, they used to be. They were some of the first books out about gay male relationships that were not just porn. They were beautifully crafted stories about couples in love, meeting and braving all kinds of odds, but always ending up happy, with lots and lots of sex. He was beyond amazed.

Lance spoke up, with a question, "Who's T. R. Tremaine?"

Keen went on to tell him who Tremaine was and what the books had meant to him. He promised to let Lance read his then turned to Phoebe and said, "Yes, I'd love to have you autograph mine."

"I'd be happy to. I'm so glad you enjoyed them."

"Why aren't you rich? I know these sold well and—"

"How many do you have?" she interrupted.

"Nine," he quickly responded.

"That's all there were. Remember, this was back in the old days. Not a lot of people would buy them or admit it. It was hard to get them marketed. And, well, life then bills took up all of it."

"How do you live? What do you live on?" He hoped he didn't sound too nosey, but he was truly worried about her. And to think she was T.R. Tremaine!

"I get a little from a few sales here and there. I don't need much." She tried to sound brave and strong, but she ended up sounding sad and lonely.

"I have an idea. Why don't you come to dinner with us tonight and you can sign all my books?" He thought it was a great idea. He'd pump Sandy for some ways to help Phoebe. "I'd consider it a great favour. As a matter of fact, why don't you come back with us now and spend the day with us? We're not doing much today and we'd love to have you spend it with us." Keen honestly hoped she would.

He suddenly thought about Lance and hoped he didn't mind him breaking up their day like this. He looked over and Lance was looking at him with a little of that hero worship thing in his eyes again. Oh, no.

"Oh, I couldn't impose on you all. You're young and just getting to know each other, " she smiled knowingly at them, "and I'm sure you have better things to do than babysit an old lady."

"Please," Lance came through for him, "we'd love to have you, and I can tell Keen really wants those autographs. Come on, make his day," he pleaded with her.

"Are you sure you want to spend the day with me?" Her disbelief was real, and all the more sad for it.

"Why wouldn't we? Lance, you got anything better to do than spend the day with a sweet, smart, interesting lady?" Keen knew that Lance would step up for him. Keen was really excited to meet this writer and Lance obviously enjoyed watching him react and respond to her.

"Nope. Sounds like a good time."

"Oh, come on. You're young and gorgeous and probably have a lot more interesting things to do." She evidently still couldn't believe what was going on.

"Phoebe," Keen got her attention. "I would've thought the same thing at first. But, Lance is not your usual young man. He's a lot more settled and serious than you'd expect." He winked at Lance as he extolled his virtues. "He's young and good looking, but he's not like the people you're probably used to seeing around here."

She actually snorted at that. "You got that right," she muttered. She looked back and forth between them then she must have decided it would be stupid to say no to a chance to get out of here and have a bit of an adventure. All evidence pointed to her never having been one to be shy before.

"Okay, I would love to go with you." Her eyes got bright all of a sudden, like she'd just thought of something. "Let me go get something I want to take with me and freshen up a little." She looked up at Keen and smiled, sweetly. "If you don't mind waiting a few minutes."

"Not at all. Take your time." They watched her move into a back room—her bedroom, Keen figured. When she closed the door, he and Lance looked at each other.

"I know you're planning something," Lance said. "Come on, tell. I love that about you. I bet that somehow or other Phoebe's life is going to change for the better."

"I don't have it all figured out yet. I'll find out more as the day goes on. I'd already decided to check with Sandy and find out what she can tell me about how we can help her," Keen admitted.

"Man, there is nothing in her kitchen. I swear. I'm not even sure the fridge is working. There's certainly nothing in it." Lance looked appalled that she had no food in the place. "I saw some crackers and some of those little cans of meat stuff. Yuk. We could, at least, get her some good groceries. I'm gonna go see if the fridge is even cold." He went off to check on what was needed there. Keen looked around the main room. There was a small air conditioner in the window that was putting out only a little cool air. It probably needed work, maybe some Freon.

Lance came back in, and he looked even more upset with the situation.

"It works. It's on. Just empty. I snuck and peeked in the cabinets." He looked at Keen, and there was sadness and compassion there. "Very, very little there, dude. This is seriously wrong. How we gonna help without hurting her feelings?"

"We'll find a way. First, we'll stop for lunch on the way home. Somewhere nice. I'll call Sandy and Kale and tell them we have a guest for supper. We'll figure something out." He looked up as he heard her door opening. Lance sprang over to help her. She had a really large tote bag as well as her purse and was having a hard time carrying it with her cast on the other arm.

"Let me get that. Lord, what do you have in here? It weighs a ton." He laughed at her as she shook her finger at him.

"It's a secret, young man. Thank you for helping me. Are we ready to go? I don't get to go out much." She looked excited and anxious. "I'm thrilled to be going out with two such good-looking men. I feel special."

"Come on, you little flirt," Keen smiled down at her as he offered his arm. "Tell me, what were you doing on the street yesterday?"

"Oh, there is a little store close to where I was walking when that punk knocked me down. It sells a lot of gay literature. They've sold a few of my books there." She told her story as they headed down the stairs and out to the truck. "I had taken the bus and gone down to get a cheque and take it to the bank. I hate riding that bus, though." She shuddered a little, thinking about it. "There are always a lot young guys on there, and they talk so bad and seem so mean. I admit, sometimes I'm scared."

Keen wouldn't even look at Lance. He knew the look he'd find on his face if he did.

He hated to admit he didn't know that much about the elderly. He was surprised to find how well she got around and how clear her mind was. She was ninety? He hoped he was half as together as this when he reached that age.

He listened to Lance and Phoebe talking as he drove to a nice restaurant close to his house. She looked surprised to be stopping here instead of his house.

"I hope you're not too full from cake. We're ready for lunch, and this is close to home." Keen looked at her, hopefully. "You've got room for something, I hope. I've been meaning to bring Lance here. While we eat, we'll tell you how we met." He added the last to get her to agree to eat with them.

At the restaurant, they regaled her with funny anecdotes about their meeting and the subsequent chaos. They told about the trick he'd played on Sandy and how she'd thought Lance was a teenager. Phoebe laughed and came back to life right before their eyes.

It was two hours before they left. They lingered over coffee and pie and Phoebe told them some stories about what it was like to have an 'alternate lifestyle' in the fifties and sixties. She told of some of the slights, but in all, they hadn't had such a bad experience.

"We were lucky to be in a neighbourhood that had a lot of folks that were open minded. It could have been so much worse. We heard of horrible things happening," she told them, her face sad as she remembered. "We considered ourselves blessed. Today, things are so much better. I'm so glad."

"Do you have a picture of Ally?" Lance asked.

"Oh, yes. Look." She reached into her purse and pulled out a small album that was frayed around the edges. She handed it over with a smile. Keen scooted his chair over so he could look at it with Lance. It was a storybook in pictures. A lot of them were old and faded, some a bit frayed around the edges. Keen figured they had been viewed and perhaps touched often through the years. There were pictures of the two of them as beautiful young women, some with their arms around each other. A lot of them were the kind that teachers had made each year and showed an age progression. Through all of them, there was a sense of happiness contentment with their lives.

"Phoebe, you're beautiful now," Keen said, loving the blush on her cheeks, "but honey, you were just gorgeous. No wonder Ally loved you so much. She was quite a looker, too. You made a striking couple."

They flipped the pages slowly, taking care and looking at each picture that showed the progression of the women's lives. Through the years, their love for each other was so apparent in the photos. The last one was taken in a hospital. Ally had no hair and her eyes were dark and hollow-looking, but she was smiling with Phoebe's arm around her.

Keen tried not to be sad. She had put this in with the others because it was part of her life. He understood that. She was something else.

Lance handed it back, and she reverently put it back into her purse. They headed to the house and were happy to see that Kale and Sandy there. Keen smiled as he witnessed a scene much like the one when he'd washed his Suburban and Sandy had watched him. Kale was in cut offs and no shirt and scrubbed her car's hubcaps as she looked at him with obvious lust in her eyes.

Keen pulled the Suburban up beside her car and rolled down the window to ask, "Gonna do mine next?"

"Sure. Leave the keys and roll the windows up tight," Kale answered.

Keen could tell that made Sandy happy. She was enjoying the show as she had that day. He and Lance helped Phoebe out and took her over to introduce her to the others.

Kale straightened up and said, "I'm sorry to be such a mess. It's nice to meet you, Miss Phoebe."

"Oh honey, don't apologise. You look good enough to eat, I swear." She laughed at everybody's expressions.

"Hey, I'm old, but not blind. I'd know you were Keen's brother anywhere. Sandy, you have a wonderful younger brother. I know you're proud of him."

Sandy replied, "I really am. I have an idea. Why don't I take your things in? We'll get a couple of chairs, let Keen and Lance help Kale, and we'll watch the show."

"I like the way you think, young lady. Let's do just that." They went into the house like the best of friends and came back out with two lawn chairs. Sandy set them up, and they sat close so they could talk. Keen and Lance looked at each other and laughed. They headed inside to find some shorts and, of course, left their chests bare.

The three men put on a great show for the girls who were both watching avidly. It was an afternoon full of fun. By the time, they were finished they were all good friends. The girls had spent the time talking together in between catcalls and wolf whistles, to which the men had preened and shown off for them.

When both vehicles were shiny and dry and the boys were shiny and wet, they stalking towards the girls. Sandy screamed and took Phoebe's hand then led her inside to safety before the grungy, wet trio could get hold of them. The three men laughed and went inside, heading for the bathrooms. Keen and Lance were on their best behaviour, all three taking separate showers quickly.

They found Sandy and Phoebe in the kitchen working on dinner preparations. Sandy was preparing a marinade for the chicken they were going to grill. Phoebe was sitting at the table, cutting vegetables for a salad.

"Well, hey, girls, anything we can do to help?" Kale asked as he went to Sandy for a quick kiss.

"Nah, your time comes later. You all get to beat your chest and work over the meat outside. We'll take care of the other stuff. Can I get a request for dessert?" She laughed when she got three. Chocolate cake with chocolate icing from Lance. Strawberry pie from Kale. Hot fudge sundaes from Keen. She'd known that one was coming. She and Phoebe looked at each other and shook their heads. Sandy went over and whispered in her ear. Phoebe smiled and nodded.

"Guys, Phoebe and I are going to go out for a few minutes. I forgot something. You all can watch TV or whatever 'til we get back. By then, the meat will be ready for you to cook and we'll start on supper. Okay?"

She had something up her sleeve. She had that look.

"Okay, what's up? She's cool, but what's the story?" Kale asked Keen and Lance after the women left.

Keen and Lance told him about all of it then they talked about ways they could help, things they could do. Lance said he would never want to make her feel like a charity case, but she needed help. Keen wanted to talk to Sandy. He had to admit this was not an area with which he was familiar. Surely there were programmes that would help. All three agreed to look into it then settled in front of the TV for a game.

Before long, glances between Lance and Keen got longer and hotter, and Kale just grinned as they got up and headed for the bedroom.

"We don't even know how long we have, but I had to have some time with you," Keen said as he pulled Lance into the room, closed the door and locked it.

"I hear ya," Lance said, going right into Keen's arms and offering up his lips. They leant on the wall next to the door. Keen knew they couldn't take a chance on going to the bed, so they would just make the most of the time they had. He figured neither wanted to get caught in the middle of something heavy, though wondrously enjoyable, and have to stop abruptly.

"Love your mouth…" Lance muttered against it.

Keen continued to use it in ways that made Lance moan.

"I want to crawl right inside you and never come out."

Keen licked across Lance's luscious lips and teased inside and back out, repeatedly. He loved that Lance was impatient for him to deepen the kiss. Lance pressed hard against Keen and had both arms wrapped around his neck, holding him tight.

"Please…come on…" Lance managed to get out, trying to push harder into Keen's open mouth. Giving in to what they both wanted, Keen thrust his tongue into Lance's mouth and swept through roughly, taking no prisoners. He began to move in and out, and Lance kept up with him, driving right back into his mouth. They were like dancers, moving together, knowing when to switch leads and move from slow to faster and harder. They were both breathing hard and their lower bodies were welded together. Keen was sure he could come just from the pressure of his dick pressing so hard against Lance's. He eased up and put his hand on Lance's head, pulling it away and into his neck.

"Breathe, baby," he whispered into Lance's ear as he tried to calm them both down. When Lance tried to pull back and look at him, he just held him tighter and rubbed his hand on the back of Lance's neck. Soothing.

Finally, Lance turned and kissed his neck, licking a path up to his ear. "Turn me loose, evil man," he whispered, blowing a soft breath into Keen's ear and smiling as Keen shuddered.

Keen's arms loosened, and he gasped as Lance dropped down and had his pants unzipped and open in seconds.

Oh. Oh my. He rested his buttocks against the wall and held onto Lance's head. Lance took him deep into his mouth and began to make him moan and sigh in delight. Keen rocked his hips back and forth, taking Lance's mouth in an attempt to ease the fire in his loins. Lance teased the tip of his cock and moved just in time to miss the jets of cum that landed harmlessly on the floor. He glanced up and smiled at Keen.

Keen looked down at him, slightly dazed. He crooked his finger, telling Lance to come back up to him. Lance shook his head and moved over to the bathroom and came back with a wet cloth to clean him then the floor. He tossed it back into the room then took Keen into his arms and kissed him.

"You're marvellous, you know that, right?" Keen asked, nuzzling right into Lance's neck, leaving little nibbling kisses.

"Thanks," Lance replied and went for Keen's mouth again. Keen gave him what he wanted, and they were again locked in a sweet, wet dance. Keen reached down and smoothed his hand over Lance's cock. He kept his tongue moving against Lance while he managed to unzip him and take him firmly in hand. Lance jerked and pushed into his hand, wanting more and harder. Keen complied and began to caress him into shuddering completion. They rested their heads together and smiled.

"Wish we could just lie down. Feel all droopy now," Lance mumbled.

Keen smiled and led him to the bathroom and proceeded to clean him up. He drew him towards the bed and pushed him down. He went to swipe the cloth across the floor again and sent it sailing back into the bathroom. He crawled up beside Lance and took him into his arms.

"Nap. I gotcha."

Lance snuggled in and drifted off within minutes. Keen held him and smoothed his hand over Lance's back, thinking about their day, about Phoebe, and what they might be able to arrange for her.

A bit later, he heard car doors slamming and woke Lance. They got up and headed into the front room. Sandy and Phoebe were already in the kitchen so they trailed in there to see what the trip had been all about. There was no evidence to show where the ladies had gone. Weird.

Kale was coming in from the deck so they went to him to see what they needed to do to help with supper.

Keen and Kale manned the grill, and Lance stayed in and helped the women while Sandy and Phoebe talked like a couple of girls. .

"It's like there's not even an age difference between you two. I'm revising everything I've ever thought about older people. I'm sure that you're unique, Phoebe, 'cause there probably aren't many ninety-year-old ladies who know who Beyoncé is, think Clooney is 'beyond gorgeous', consider Justin Timberlake 'a very smart young man' and wonder what that nice young Barack would do next."

"Oh, go on. I've always watched television. I like to keep up with what's going on in the world. There's no excuse for being ignorant in this day and age." Well, that pretty much said it all.

With all of them working together in their respective areas, supper was fabulous. Conversation flowed from one subject to the other with everyone contributing despite being a varied group who'd come together from different ages and areas. Keen was happy they meshed so well. They all laughed and teased as they cleared the table after the meal.

"Hey, what's for dessert?" Keen asked, remembering they'd talked about it but not seeing anything.

"Gee, I don't know. You all wanted something different, so we didn't know what to do," Sandy said.

"That's okay," said Lance, trying not to sound disappointed.

"Shit, don't believe it. I know her, and she's not about to have a big meal without a dessert. Come on, Sandy, 'fess up," Keen said, laughing as she blushed at being caught in the lie. She and Phoebe got up and went to the pantry and came back with two big boxes.

"You all go on in and get settled in the living room. Phoebe and I will get dessert ready. Coffee all around?" she asked, and they all agreed. She fixed decaf, and she and Phoebe giggled as they prepared the individual desserts.

Phoebe went in and sat on the couch with Keen and Lance, and Sandy carried in a large tray with chocolate cake, strawberry pie, a hot fudge sundae, key lime pie, and a big brownie on it.

Lance jumped up to take it from her.

"Wicked!" he exclaimed as he passed it around so each could get their preference. Sandy went back for the coffee and Kale went to help her bring it in. They sat around in the living room and there were sounds of happy feasting as they devoured the desserts. There wasn't much conversation as they finished their treats.

Keen looked over to find that Phoebe was sitting quietly, with tears rolling down her face. Not wanting to embarrass her, he leant over her to ask, quietly, "You okay, honey?"

She nodded and handed him the plate from her lap where she'd been using her good hand to eat the key lime pie. He took it and leaned to shield her a little so the others wouldn't see her as she dried the tears on her face.

"Thank you, darling boy." She patted his shoulder to let him know it was okay to move. Sandy gathered the dishes, and Kale got up to help, leaving Keen and Lance flanking Phoebe on the couch.

"What is it, hon? Does your arm hurt?" Lance asked, clearly wanting to make her more comfortable.

"No, it's silly. I'm just so happy." She laughed, a little embarrassed. "I haven't had this good a time in years. I can't believe how nice you all have been to me. This has been a wonderful day." The sentence that was unspoken seemed as loud as the one that was heard. I wish I didn't have to go back home.

"Hey, we've enjoyed it as much as you have. You don't have to act like we're doing you a favour." Keen wanted her to know she was important. She needed to know there was a place for her. He vowed to find out where it was. It certainly wasn't in that dump where she lived. "Can I ask you something?" he broached.

"Sure."

"I don't want to hurt your feelings or make you feel bad, but I can't stand the way you're living. I want to see if there isn't something that can be done to improve your life a little." He stopped to look at her, hoping she wasn't angry.

"Oh. Oh, I don't know what to say," Phoebe said, tearing up again. "I can't believe this is happening. I've been alone and broke for so long. I live the best life I can, but I worry all the time about safety."

"Phoebe, please don't be upset with me. I know it's none of my business," Keen paused and looked to Lance for help.

Lance cut in and said, "We think you're a wonderful lady. We want you to be safe and happy. I'll use the fact that I'm the youngest here to say it like it is. There's not enough food in your place. It's not safe where you live. Your air isn't working right. I hope I'm not being too rude, but I don't know how else to say it. We're worried about you. We like you. We want to help change a few things for you."

"That's the nicest thing I've ever heard," Phoebe said, looking back and forth between them. "You're like my two white knights. I know it's silly, but that's how I think of you. Now, I know it's deplorable. I came from better. I've lived better. That is just how things are now. I haven't got the money for anything better. I might even lose that place if I don't..." She stopped as she realised what she'd almost revealed.

"Finish that sentence, please, Miss Phoebe." Keen said, looking sternly at her.

"Don't try to browbeat me, young man. Yes, I'm behind on the rent and have been told if I don't come up with it, I'll be put out." She looked down at her lap, hiding her eyes from them.

"That would probably be a good thing," Keen started to say just as Sandy and Kale walked back in the room.

"What's the matter? Something's wrong, I can tell," Sandy said, coming over and kneeling in front of Phoebe.

That started a big discussion of Phoebe's current situation and ways to make things better for her. The conversation went round and round with ideas coming from all sides. All of it took lots of money, and she refused to take any from them. Keen wanted to know about programmes that might help, knowing that Phoebe didn't want charity.

Lance spoke up, "I've got a sort of idea."

They all stopped and looked at him, waiting.

"If I understand things correctly, Kale might be spending his nights over at Sandy's." He looked at them and they both nodded. "I know I'm hoping to be spending my nights in Keen's room. I don't think that's news to anybody." Again, they all nodded, still waiting for the punch line.

"Why can't Phoebe move in here for a while, in Kale's room, at least 'til we can figure something out?"

The others all spoke at once.

"You're a fucking genius!"

"Oh, I couldn't."

"Lance, what a great idea."

"That's my man," Keen said.

Okay, so it was a good plan. Now they had to convince Phoebe.

Keen took the lead. "Why can't you?"

"You can't just open your home to me after knowing me for just a couple of days. It…it's just not done. What if I made you crazy? I'm old. I'll cramp your style." She tried to think of other things, but her expression showed that the idea of not having to go back to her home began to sink in. She stopped and looked at them all. "I don't know what to think."

Sandy took over. She found out that Phoebe was only on one medication that she took in the mornings and she had some in her purse. Good. There was certainly no one who would miss her tonight so Sandy was going home to get a gown for Phoebe to sleep in.

Keen, Kale, and Lance would move the very few things she wanted from her place tomorrow and they would pay up her back rent. When she started to object, Keen said,

"Phoebe, I'd pay that much for one autograph on one book. You're going to give me nine. Consider us well past even."

She blushed.

"What are you talking about?" Sandy asked, confused.

Keen explained about Phoebe turning out to be his favourite author and how she'd promised to sign all his books.

"Lance, honey, would you go over and get me my tote now?" Phoebe asked.

Lance hopped up and got it, exaggerating how heavy it was, though not by much.

When he was seated again, she looked around at all of them, making eye contact with each before she said, "I'm going to do something now that's going to make me very happy. You're the best group of people I've met in years. You've made me so happy today." Her voice shook a little, but she went on. "I never thought I'd feel so good again. I have something for Keen." She looked at him and saw the surprise on his face.

"In here are my original, hand-written copies of all nine of the books you have. I'm giving them to you." She watched his face, seeing shock and disbelief.

"Oh my God, you can't. You're serious?" Keen couldn't believe it. He would be thrilled, and couldn't wait to see them. He grasped the tote as she gestured for him to take it. He reached in and pulled one out. It was the first one. Oh, he could not believe he was holding T. R. Tremaine's first novel in his hand—the original. He felt tears in his eyes.

"Uh, I have another idea," Lance spoke up again.

"Go for it," Sandy said, obviously proud of the one he'd had earlier.

"Wouldn't they be worth, like, a lot of money?" he asked hesitantly. "I know how much they mean to Keen. Maybe you could make copies of them, sign them and give those to Keen but sell these for a lot of money. If they were as popular as Keen said, I bet you could get a mint for them."

There was stunned silence. Keen looked at him with a look of dawning joy. Phoebe looked at him, doubtfully. Kale and Sandy were clearly just sort of wondering about it all.

"Do you really think…?" Phoebe began, but Keen stopped her.

"That's brilliant. I repeat, that's my man," He leant over and took a quick kiss. Phoebe put both hands up to her mouth and giggled like a little girl.

"Cute, aren't they?" Kale said, winking at her.

"Do you really think…?" she repeated, not believing it.

Lance smiled over at her. "Let me look around on the net. Keen and I will both work on it. I bet we can find a way to make you one rich old lady."

She smiled back at him. "Now wouldn't that be a kick in the head?"

"Phoebe, I'll never forget that you offered these to me. That means more than you'll ever know," Keen said, leaning over to take a quick kiss from her, too. "I would like to make a copy of them and have you sign them. They'll be my prized possessions." He took more out and shook his head as he saw each beloved title.

"I'll be glad to, sweet boy. I had the idea as we were leaving my apartment. What else am I going to do with them? This way someone would have them who loved them. That thought makes me happy."

"Oh, Phoebe," Keen said, reverently.

"Are you sure you wouldn't rather keep the originals yourself? I gave them to you," Phoebe asked Keen.

"No way, I'm giving them back." He made decisions as he talked to her. "As a matter of fact, I'm taking them tomorrow and copying them then putting them in a bank vault for safekeeping 'til we decide the best way to use them for you."

Keen noticed her looking a little tired. He put the books back in the tote and set it behind the couch for now. He looked over at Sandy, and she nodded. She went out the door to get a gown and other things for Phoebe to be comfortable tonight. Kale headed to his room to pack a few things, turning the room from his to hers.

While all this was going on, Lance decided to entertain Phoebe before she went to bed. He muttered something to Keen, and he smiled and nodded. They got up and helped her up from the couch.

"Come on," Keen said to her. "While they get everything ready, how would you like to watch Lance do a nice relaxing tai chi routine? I'll get him to show you some of his fantastic moves tomorrow, but this might be nice for tonight."

"Oh, I'd love it. I've always wanted to do that. I've seen it, and it's so beautiful." Phoebe sounded pleased at getting a chance to see it up close.

"I'll be glad to teach you," Lance said, as they entered the work out room.

"Oh no, I'm too old," she said.

"Not at all. I promise you can do it. I'm going to start teaching at the dojo down from Keen's gym soon, and we'll have classes. You can be my first student," he smiled at her and took up a position on the mat. "It's nicer with music, but I'll just show you a slow one-hundred-eight movement. It's not too long and it's all about concentration and relaxation. The benefits are many, and include flexibility, increased circulation and stress reduction. You might enjoy watching and even learning it."

Keen and Phoebe sat on the weight bench and watched, both entranced by the beauty of Lance's movements. Slow, fluid, and graceful. He seemed to be unaware of them as he progressed through the movements, some repeating in different places. There were turns and glides and even some high kicks, but all with such a gentle flow that made them look like dance. When he stopped, he saw that Sandy and Kale stood in the doorway watching, too. He bowed and went to Phoebe.

"For you," he said and kissed her cheek.

"I feel like it's Christmas. That was lovely," she said to Lance. "I'd love to try to learn just some of it…if you really think I could." She still looked sceptical.

"I promise you can."

Chapter Seven

After Sandy had gotten Phoebe settled, Keen and Lance headed for the computer, eager to do some research on her books. Keen knew he wasn't the only one who had collected all her books religiously. They meant a lot to him, and he figured she probably had a following.

Keen got more excited as the possibilities presented themselves to him. "You know, I bet that they would sell really well again if the right person got hold of them and marketed them in the right way. They really were record breaking when they came out. There was very little out there in this genre. I can't wait for you to read them. They're wonderful."

"I'll start the first one tomorrow, if there's time. Hey, look, here they are." Lance drew Keen's eyes to the screen where a list of her books and a short bio were shown.

"Where'd you find it?" Keen asked.

"Just typed in her name in the search engine, and it came up. It's not a good site, just lists of books and authors."

"We'll look for more. I'm glad I've got you to help. I'm glad you're into computers, too. Between us, we'll find what we need."

Lance shrugged. "Do you think we could come up with a marketing campaign that would get them out there again then make a big splash with the sale of the originals? I don't want to sound like a jerk, but it has a bit of urgency to it, don't you think? I mean, she's ninety, she needs it soon, so she can enjoy it."

"Yeah, I know what you mean." Keen rubbed Lance's neck as they talked, just keeping a hand on him and enjoying the feel of the muscles in his neck and shoulders. "I know a couple of guys who work at a publishing company. I'll give Ron a call tomorrow and see what he thinks of the idea."

"Great!"

Keen's eyes brightened as he remembered his friend. "He's gay, and we've talked a little about literature. Come to think of if, we've even mentioned these books. He may know enough to send us in the right direction."

"Mmm…" Lance hummed as he moved back into Keen's absentminded caresses. "You ready for bed? I hope it was all right to assume I'd be over here with you. I just sort of blurted it out. I didn't mean to…" He paused and looked up at Keen, afraid he'd overstepped.

Keen's lips stopped the rest as if to say "Shut up, Stupid." He kept their lips locked as he turned the computer chair and pulled Lance right up into his arms. They pressed together in what was becoming a favoured position. They fit so well in so many ways. Physically was one of the best.

Lance wasn't slow to give up on the stupidity and jump right in. He had both arms tight around Keen's neck and held on as he rubbed his cock against Keen's.

"Damn," Keen muttered.

"Mmm?"

"We were gonna get tested so we could..." His words disappeared into Lance's mouth again. Right. Later. They'd keep up the safety routine, but he was really looking forward to being able to feel Lance without the rubbers. He admonished himself to stop whining and get busy with his man.

"Let's go to bed," Keen suggested, reaching down to go through a few quick clicks to turn off the computer then pulling Lance towards 'their' room.

When they got to the room, Lance turned to Keen and asked, "She can't hear us, can she? I mean, uh...I feel weird..." He trailed off as Keen chuckled.

"She may be here for a little while. You wanna give up sex?" He almost laughed out loud at the look of horror on Lance's face at that.

"Not."

"Besides, after you read her books, you won't worry about her hearing us, not that I think she can. She knows all about guys and sex, believe me."

"Wow. That just blows my mind, ya know? That little old lady writes about gay sex?" Lance's expression clearly showed his amazement.

"Wrote, hon, wrote. When she was much younger. A lot of gay literature is written by women. You'd be surprised. Have you ever read any books, fiction, actual stories about couples and their lives?" Keen started to undress Lance as he talked.

"No. I guess I didn't even know such things existed," Lance admitted. "I feel stupid again. I don't really care for porn, which is all I heard about from a lot of my friends back home." He unconsciously moved around to facilitate Keen's mission. "But I think I'd like to read her books. I like the idea of gay *love* stories. That's so cool." He looked down at Keen kneeling before him. "Uh, can I help you with that?" He laughed as Keen untied his sneakers and pulled one leg up at a time to slide his pants down. Lance held onto his shoulder for balance.

"Nope, got it covered," Keen replied, looking up at him. "You can return the favour, though."

"Not a problem. Come back up here." Lance pulled him up and proceeded to remove the man's clothes quickly then they turned to the bed together.

"Anything you want to do, baby?" Keen asked, tugging Lance in beside him and turning to face him. "Something you like that we haven't done?" He leant in and took a kiss, smiling as Lance's arms surrounded him and he deepened the kiss.

"You mean we've already done all there is?" Lance pretended to pout then laughed. "Mmm…it's all good with you," he murmured against Keen's lips.

"I want to watch your face while I fuck you, long, slow, and deep." Keen pulled back, watching as Lance's face turned red at his words. "I want to put your legs over my shoulders and lean in and fuck that hot mouth with mine at the same time. Sound good to you?" He followed his question with a long, wet lick across Lance's collarbone from one side to the other, pausing to suck a little right over his rapid heartbeat.

Lance's answer was to push Keen over so he could reach past him to the nightstand. He grabbed the oil and another sheath. He yelped as Keen put his hands on his ribs and rubbed, tickling him as he eased back over him.

Lance laughed and dropped his goodies on the bed and attacked right back. They rolled around, laughing and rubbing.

"What a hoot. With you...I'm finding out that...sex can be fun." Lance had a hard time getting the words out between giggles. "It's not just in and out and 'Oh, that feels good'. That tickles me...that, too, I mean..." he said, somewhere between a snort and another giggle.

"I'm glad you're...tickled."

"Uncle...I give...stop, Keen," he gasped out between bouts of laughter. "You're gonna wear me out just from laughing then I won't have any energy to stay up late and make you the happiest man on earth."

Keen immediately stopped and put his hands up. "Why didn't you say so?"

Lance smiled at him and pointed a finger. "I never got the chance. You didn't think I was gonna forget you, did you?" He leant back into Keen and put his tongue flat against his right nipple and licked. He went around and around it then took it into his mouth and sucked hard, pulling Keen up from the bed, gasping and bowing his back. He was a fair man, so he did the same to the other side, getting about the same response. He looked down at Keen and smiled smugly.

"Lie down," Keen whispered to him. Oh. Now that was sexy. All playing was over and it was time to get down to the business of loving. Lance was all about that. He followed orders, looking around for the condom and the oil he'd gotten earlier.

He handed it over then took the bottle back from Keen.

Keen raised his brows, and Lance just smiled at him, taking the top off and slicking up two fingers. Keen's eyes widened as realisation hit him. *Oh, fuck me*, he thought. Lance was going to…

Lance leaned up a little to one side and raised his knee. He reached down with his fingers and very slowly eased them into his hole. Keen thought he'd have a heart attack. Lance never took his eyes off Keen's as he moved his long fingers in and out, pushing them deep. He whispered to Keen, "Help me. Put one of yours in, too."

Oh, God.

Keen reached for the oil and soon he had moved down to place his index finger beside Lance's. He began to ease it in, not wanting to hurt him. This was one he'd never done. Just watching Lance finger himself to get ready for him had been the sexiest thing he'd seen in…forever. He pushed on in, feeling Lance's wet fingers beside his as they both began to move in and out. He heard Lance breathe faster.

He leant down to take his mouth. Lance was ready, mouth open and eager. They met roughly and pushed against each other. Their tongues clashed and moved around, swirling and tangling. Keen pulled away to rake his tongue over Lance's lips then returned to play inside his mouth.

"More…" Lance begged, pushing against his hand and against his mouth. Keen removed his finger and placed it on the inside of Lance's, pushing in to hit Lance's gland. Liking the fact that they were working together to prepare Lance for him, Keen reached for that sweet spot again. He took the rough sound Lance made into his mouth and moved in again to get the same response. He finally deemed Lance ready.

"Cover me," he said against Lance's ear. Keen swore he heard Lance whimper as he grabbed the condom with the other hand. Lance put it up to his mouth and tore off the end of the wrapper. They both used their free hands to smooth it on. Keen almost came right then.

Keen eased back a second, taking away some of the stimulus, easing his finger out of Lance and settling him onto the bed. He reached to take Lance's hand and gently pull out his fingers. Keen pulled it up and kissed the back of Lance's hand, a tribute to the sexy foreplay Lance had provided them.

Keen settled between Lance's legs, scooting up a little, his knees flush against Lance. He took Lance's knees and pushed his legs up and out, resting them on his shoulders. He reached to spread those cheeks then he eased into Lance, looking into his eyes the whole time. This wasn't something he did to him, but with him.

Keen pushed until he was all the way to the hilt. He pulled back just a little and pushed in again a little harder. Lance grunted with that and smiled. He liked it. Keen did it a few more times with short, quick thrusts moving Lance on the bed each time. Then he pulled nearly completely out and rammed all the way in. Lance opened his mouth to cry out and Keen bent far forward to take the sound.

Keen put his hands on Lance's hips and held him as he continued to thrust in and out, the tops of his thighs slapping Lance's buttocks as he came all the way against him each time. Lance's arms were trying to hold Keen's shoulders against him so he could keep on kissing him, but Keen wanted to pull away a little and see Lance's face.

"Fuck me, Keen, you…" Lance couldn't put his thoughts together. He tried again, "More…harder. God, you're the sexiest thing I've ever…Oh!" He tried to raise his head from the bed to get to Keen. "Do that again…please."

Keen pushed in to peg his gland again and again then put his mouth to Lance's and began to fuck it as he'd promised. Soon Lance was a shivering, twisting, sweating mass of sensation. That had been Keen's plan. He kissed him roughly, forcefully, as he continued the hard thrusting with his hips.

Soon, he couldn't hold out any longer. The rush came all the way from his toes in waves of aching fulfilment. He came in great pulses, filling the condom deep inside Lance. He pulled his mouth away, throwing back his head and biting his lip to keep from yelling out.

Lance followed him into ecstasy. They shuddered and shimmered and quaked until they finally came down and Keen let Lance's legs. He eased out, took care of the condom then fell beside Lance, breathing hard.

Lance pulled him close and kissed him all over his face and neck, shoulders and chest. Short, sweet kisses told Keen he was deeply cared for. He smiled as it seemed that Lance didn't intend to miss a spot.

"Hey."

"Hmm?" Lance didn't even look up. He was on a mission.

"Come back up here, baby?" he asked, as Lance was now down to his stomach, moving slowly and covering the area with soft loving kisses.

Lance came back up there. He rested on one elbow and gazed down at Keen.

"You totally blew me away, man. Totally." Lance just looked at him, obviously trying to put something into words. Keen waited.

"I've done most of this stuff before, sort of. With you, it's like it's more, ya know? Everything feels so much stronger. I know, I've said that before. Hell, I can't get it out right." He shook his head, clearly frustrated at not being able to get what he was feeling across like he wanted to.

"Lance, look at me, honey." Keen took his face between his hands for a second before he said, "I think...I won't say for sure yet, but I think I'm falling in love with you." He looked right into his eyes and waited a minute to see if Lance would freak out. Nope. "I know what you're saying. Don't worry about saying it right. The intensity of feelings comes from the way we feel about each other to begin with. It makes things...better. You agree with that?"

Lance nodded, turning his face and kissing Keen's palm. "Yeah, I know. It seems like we've known each other forever and I feel strongly about you. I've never been in love, but I think this is probably what it feels like." He kissed Keen's other palm and rubbed his cheek against his hands. Leaning down, he kissed Keen softly on the lips, back and forth.

"Nice," Keen murmured.

"I can tell you this," Lance said, certainty in his voice. "I'm not going back to Hawaii. I want to stay here with you as long as you'll have me. I want to see if this is really...what it is." He blushed after admitting his desire and his plan.

He was pulled down and hugged hard against Keen's chest. Keen's face was in his neck and Lance heard him say, "Thank God."

* * * *

The next morning, Keen woke to wonderful smells coming from his kitchen. He glanced over and saw that Lance was still sleeping soundly beside him. He smiled. They'd made love again last night after *almost* professing to love each other. He had no doubt he was in love with Lance. He just hadn't wanted to say too much too soon and scare him. It was early in their relationship, but…well, he knew…what it was.

He eased out of bed, covering Lance and leaning to put a kiss on the back of his neck. He showered, dressed then left the room, all without waking his lover. He was going to check out the smells coming from the kitchen. Was that coffee? He walked a little faster.

"Good morning, sweet boy." Phoebe turned from taking some kind of homemade cinnamon rolls out of the oven. "I hope you don't mind. I got nosey and found all kinds of things I could make for you all."

"Honey, why would I mind? It smells like heaven in here." He was a sucker for a breakfast pastry of any kind. "You didn't have to get up and cook for us. You're here as a guest…" He trailed off into blissful sounds as he tasted the hot roll he'd snatched from the rack she'd placed it on. "Changed my mind. You're hired. You looking for a job?"

She laughed in delight, clearly happy she'd done something he liked so much

"I'd love to cook for you. I used to do all the cooking since I worked from home and Ally worked so hard at the school. She was a hell of a teacher. She gave a hundred and fifty percent. I haven't forgotten how to cook, just haven't had much opportunity." She stood still a moment, lost in memory, smiling.

Or funds, Keen thought.

"God, what's that fabulous smell?" They heard from behind them and turned to find Lance, stretching, arms reaching for the ceiling, shirt riding halfway up his stomach. Oops, was that a...yep, a hickey...now when had he done that?

"Looks like someone had a nice night," Phoebe said, laughing at the expression on Keen's face and the bewilderment on Lance's.

"What?" Lance asked, obviously realising he should be embarrassed about something, but not getting the joke.

"Nothing, dear boy. You hungry this morning? Want some eggs with your rolls?" she asked.

"You cooked. Cool." He headed for the rack of rolls. "Wait, should you be cooking?" He tasted one and sighed. "Yeah, you should be cooking."

Keen and Phoebe laughed. Keen suggested, "Let's all help. Lance, you do juice and coffee. Phoebe, how do you like yours?" He looked over at her then leaned to give her a quick hug, liking having her there with them.

"I'll do the eggs. Scrambled, with cheese, okay with everyone?"

They all got busy and before long were sitting down to a wonderful breakfast. They talked about the day's activities. It was decided that Phoebe and the three men would go to her place and clean it out, there not being much to retrieve. They would have Sandy check into what kinds of programmes were available for Phoebe to get some assistance.

Once she was moved in, they would all brainstorm about the books and originals. Keen was going to get them copied, call Ron and see what might be done with them then he and Lance were going to the clinic to get tested. Whew. It would be a busy day.

Sandy and Kale came over, and they took both vehicles and everyone went to Phoebe's. Keen was glad they'd get a chance to see the way Phoebe had been living. He and Sandy made eye contact several times as they packed Phoebe's few belongings and got out of there as quickly as possible. Keen stopped in and paid her back rent then they all left with a sigh of relief.

"Keen, I'm happy being with you and Lance, but I don't intend to stay there. I'm not going to cramp your style, boys, and don't say I wouldn't," she said, as she saw them both start to shake their heads. "You need to be able to walk around however you want to in your own home. We need to find me a place for old folks that I can afford," she ended, determinedly.

"We'll cross that bridge when we come to it," Keen said. He knew she was right, but that wasn't his priority right now. They drove back to the house where he let Sandy and Kale got her settled while he and Lance took care of other business.

They group met for supper that night. Sandy and Phoebe had cooked a great meal, and Kale had worked on getting the room fixed the way Sandy had suggested for Phoebe to be comfortable. Keen and Lance both had tiny bruises on their arms from the blood test earlier. Keen related his conversation with Ron.

Ron agreed the time was right to reintroduce T. R. Tremaine's works. There was now such a great market for them. It was a shame that no one had advised Phoebe about the opportunity before now. Ron was sure they would be very successful. They would copy the originals as suggested and plan for a big event to auction the real ones. He felt safe in saying that she'd make enough to live out her life. That was what they hoped.

Phoebe sat and listened.

"I'm amazed that the work I did earlier is going to be reissued and might help me more now. You've all done so much for me. Every time I think about how wonderful you all are, I want to just cry."

"Phoebe?" Lance said, worry in his voice.

"Hush now. I'm just a little overwhelmed at all this. I can't believe that just a couple of days ago I didn't know any of you and my life was...well, it was pretty bleak. There's no way I can ever thank you. I wish there was something I could do..." She looked around the table at the people who in such a short time had done so much for her.

"I have an idea," Lance said.

They all paused. He'd proven to have really good ideas.

"You could just make cinnamon rolls in the mornings. That would make it pretty much even as far as I'm concerned." He sounded so serious. They all burst out laughing. Leave it to Lance to put things into perspective. She had become important to them, too. They wanted her to be happy and safe.

"It's funny, but here's a thought. While you stay with us—" Keen held up his hand to stop her from interrupting. "Wait a minute, honey. While you're here, if you want to cook a little, dust a little, just do some light stuff, we'll call it housekeeping and pay you a small amount." He knew she had to feel like she was doing her part, but he couldn't allow her to do much.

"Seriously, Phoebe, we're both going to be working. If you want to make a little spending money, you could help us out, like with breakfast this morning. Don't take on anything heavy or tiring, but it would be beneficial to all of us." Keen watched her to make sure she believed he meant it.

"You're just making that up to make me feel better, you darling man."

"Yes and no. It will make you feel better to be contributing, right?" He caught her eager nod. "We would benefit, too, because we're going to be busy with my work, Lance's new job, and working with Ron on launching your books again." When he saw she was listening to him, he went on. "Then we'll plan a big event to auction your originals. This should all take a few weeks. There's no sense in you getting a new place until you see how much you will have and where you want to be. We'll try not to embarrass you with PDAs." He had to laugh when it was Lance who blushed instead of Phoebe.

Sandy spoke up, "I would love to have you spend some time at my house, too, some of the time. That would give the two lovebirds some time alone, and we could work on some projects together."

Sandy looked appraisingly at Phoebe and said, "I've been wondering. We've been talking at work about having some people come in and work with some of the kids in the cancer ward. They have it so hard, being there all the time. Some don't have parents who can stay with them. They're scared and alone. Would you be interested?" Sandy knew from being around Phoebe that she could handle it part time. She knew Phoebe would be great with the little ones.

"That's so strange," Phoebe started.

Sandy suddenly remembered about her partner dying of cancer. Maybe it would be too hard on her. "What? I'm sorry, is it something you can't see yourself doing? I understand, it's not for everyone. I..." Sandy got no further.

"No, please. When Ally was...was dying, we both took it upon ourselves to spend time in the ward with the children. It was her affinity to the young ones, you know. She loved children. When she found that she had that awful disease then saw so many young ones there, she drew me in and we spent many, many hours with them." Phoebe looked around the table, her eyes bright with remembrance and sadness. She shook her head, sadly. "I can't believe I forgot about that. I was so caught up in my own grief that I forgot about the little ones. I'd love to go back and work with them again. Will you help me get started?" She looked at Sandy.

"I'd be happy to. We'll do it together." Sandy reached across and took Phoebe's hand and they smiled, both with tears in their eyes.

Keen and Lance looked at each other then at Kale, and they all got up at the same time.

"You ladies, go in and relax," Keen said. "We'll clean up." They hustled the two women out of the kitchen and breathed a sigh of relief.

"Way too much emotion."

Chapter Eight

It was amazing what determined people could get done in a short amount of time. Before the week was over, the Thomas household was settled into a nice routine which pleased everyone. Phoebe had breakfast ready for them when they woke up each morning, ready for work.

Lance was working with Hammer and had even been talked into training for an upcoming contest with others from their dojo. Keen was secretly looking forward to watching his man shine. He planned on taking Phoebe and Sandy to the event. Lance liked working with Hammer and had a few classes already, working with the advanced students Hammer had told him about.

Keen was back at work at the gym and checking in with his computer business. The gym pretty well took care of itself since he'd hired a great staff. He kept up with them and showed up to answer questions, have planning meetings and write cheques. He spent more time on the computer. He'd put a couple of projects on the back burner and worked a lot with Ron on getting things going for Phoebe.

He had the same programmes on the computers at home and work, so he was able to stop in at home once in a while and work there — and check on whether Phoebe was doing too much and get her ideas on their project.

"Are you excited about meeting with Ron and his publishers tomorrow?" he asked as he sat back from the computer and looked at her. Tomorrow, they would meet to finalise plans for the launch of the market campaign for her line of books. She would find out what her advance would be and maybe what she could expect from all this.

Her eyes were bright with it. He didn't have to wonder. She had already come up with some good ideas and they had gone back and forth with Ron on them.

"I'm more than excited. I won't sleep a wink tonight. I'm glad you put that little television in my room. I can watch stuff late at night when I can't sleep."

"We're not...uh...you can't...I mean..." Keen wasn't usually at a loss for words. And he didn't blush very often, either.

"No, sweetie. I can't hear you two at night." She laughed at him, good-naturedly. "I've never slept much at night, not for a long time anyway."

"Whew! Good to know. Lance would freak if he thought..."

"You all are funny. Don't worry about it. You know it makes me happy to see two people happy and in love," she said, looking up at him. "You do love that boy, don't you?"

"Yes, ma'am. I do, very much. It didn't take me long to realise it." He didn't mind telling her. He knew she understood.

"Have you told him?" She looked at him and held up her hand before adding, "I know it's none of my business. I just hope you will before long. Never take for granted that you'll have a long time."

"I understand. We've already admitted that we probably are," he told her, smiling at his hesitancy. "We kind of talked all the way around it but haven't declared it yet. I'd like to do something special for him when I tell him, ya know?"

"Has he read any of the books yet?" she asked.

"Yeah, he's read a couple, and I think he's on the third one. He loves them. He never knew there was good gay fiction out there. He's hooked." He smiled a little, thinking of how excited Lance had been when he'd finished the first book and reached for the second. He was thrilled with the story of the two men in the book and how they'd overcome obstacles to be together, despite negativity and hostility all around them.

"Why don't you pick a favourite scene in one of them and recreate it?" she suggested, shyly. "If you think he'd enjoy that."

"That's brilliant. He'd be so tickled. You know, I don't know whether to pick something from one of the first three or one that he hasn't read yet, so when he gets to it, he'll realise what I did." His mind was going a mile a minute, thinking of scenes from the stories he loved, knowing that Lance was coming to love them, too.

"Think about it, and it will come to you, dear," she said, patting him on the shoulder. "You're such a good, good man. He's lucky to have you in his life. So am I. Don't think I don't know it." She laid her head on his shoulder for a second, and he, in turn, patted her shoulder.

"We're both lucky to have you in our lives," he told her, touching her cheek gently, "and know this, whatever happens we will stay close. I can't imagine not being around you."

"You've made me so happy." She leant back and put both hands up to her mouth.

"Why don't you get some rest? We'll order in tonight, and you'll be nice and bright for the meeting tomorrow."

Keen, Lance, and Ron were talking often to discuss the originals and the best way to get the most out of them. They talked about how to go about it. Should Phoebe come forward and reveal herself as T. R. Tremaine? It certainly wouldn't hurt anyone now. There was no longer any need for anonymity. But was she ready to go through the publicity, the hype, the spin? Maybe it would be better for Lance and Keen to be there and she could tag along to observe and enjoy without the hassle. Those were some of the things being talked about nightly as the group met to discuss the day's work and the next day's plans.

Phoebe went to her room to rest. Keen went to his stack of books and picked out his favourite, number seven. All of her books had been sentimental and full of angst, heartache, heartbreak and hard lessons. Besides having great sex, they all had such heartfelt love. The men went through a lot in each book, but their love prevailed in the end and, God bless 'em, they all ended happily. He was a sucker, he knew, but he preferred a happy ending.

He skimmed through the well-worn book and had just decided on what scene in the book he would do, when he heard the door open. He was glad Lance didn't come in yelling and rouse Phoebe. Keen wanted a little time with him. He sat on the side of the bed and let Lance find him. It didn't take him long, since he was looking pretty hard.

"Hey." Keen smiled at his lanky lover.

"Hey, there you are." Lance came directly over to him, leaning down to kiss him. He bent and put his arms around Keen's neck, holding him still for a long thorough kiss. He put the whole day's worth of missing him into it.

Keen pulled him closer and eased him down to straddle his lap.

Lance looked at him. "I like this."

He scooted closer, putting his knees on the bed beside Keen's hips. He plastered their torsos together, tightening his arms around Keen's neck before going back for more mouth.

Keen licked Lance's lips, top and bottom, and pushed between them, going in for another taste. He loved Lance's mouth. Loved it, craved it. He sipped and nipped and tangled tongues with Lance until his breath came rapidly and his heart thumped in his chest.

"Welcome home," Keen chuckled when he was finally able to draw a good mouthful of air. Lance laughed with him. Keen fell back on the bed, taking Lance with him and they rolled.

"It never occurred to me I could miss someone so much in just a few hours," Lance admitted as they ended with him lying on top of Keen, looking down at him. "I can't stop wanting you. It's crazy. I think about you all the time," he said, shaking his head a little,

Keen reached up with both hands to enclose Lance's face and hold it still for him. "Honey, you seem to be under the impression you're alone in this." He pulled him down for a quick swipe over his lips with an agile tongue. "Silly boy, it's the same for me. Isn't it great?" He pulled him down again, this time for more than a swipe. He lingered over it, tasting and sucking Lance's tongue into his mouth.

"Uh, where's Phoebe?" Lance remembered and pulled back, worried about finishing what they'd started.

Keen smiled up at him. "She's resting in her room. We're ordering out tonight. She has a big day tomorrow. We have a big night tonight, starting now." Keen kissed him again, long, hot, and hungry.

Relaxing, Lance began pulling at their clothes, obviously wanting to get to skin. Keen helped, and it wasn't long before they were naked and trying to get closer than they were, not really possible, but the attempt was fun.

Lance must have decided to go back to class. Having passed 'Keen's Cock 101' with flying colours, he'd now enroled in 'Rimming Keen' class.

He leant down to Keen and whispered, "Turn over for me." Keen looked into his eyes for a second then turned for him. He settled on his stomach. He groaned as Lance began a thorough massage of his back and shoulders. The man had fabulous hands. He closed his eyes and soaked up the sensations as Lance's hands moved over him.

Lance leaned over him and made the same trip over his back with his lips. He moved them on down to Keen's ass. He kissed each cheek playfully, smiling as Keen pushed them up to him, asking for more. Lance pulled a pillow down and pulled up with the other hand on Keen's hip, urging him to rise and let him slip it under him. After getting Keen positioned the way he wanted it, Lance set about practicing for the final exam.

He slid further back, spread Keen's legs and bent to his task. Lance looked at the tight hole between Keen's cheeks, leaned and blew on it. It twitched in response. Putting his tongue to Keen, he began to move it around and around the hole then pushed down hard as Keen pushed up against him.

Keen moaned as Lance plied his tongue over and over. Lance held Keen's cheeks wide and pointed his tongue and thrust it into the quivering hole. Keen clenched tightly and held Lance's tongue prisoner for a moment. When Lance pushed further then began a rhythmic thrusting, Keen yelled into the other pillow.

Lance kept it up as long as he could, and Keen loved it. Lance reached under Keen to take his prick in hand. A couple of jerks and he was coming against the pillow. Lance eased back from him and kissed each cheek again, running his tired tongue up Keen's back to his neck. He kissed him repeatedly, reaching a hand up to move it through his hair.

"My God, that was…unbelievable." Keen could barely speak. He made a monumental effort and turned, pulled out the pillow then took Lance into his arms. He squeezed hard, wanting to pull him right into his pores. He couldn't get close enough. Lance groaned a little as his ribs were squinched.

"Sorry…I just…" Keen put his hand up to Lance's face again and held it for his perusal. Lance looked smug, obviously knowing he'd pleased Keen.

"What can I do for you now, lover?" Keen wanted to make him feel just as loved. He reached up for a kiss, taking Lance's mouth hard, sucking his tongue into his mouth to tease and tangle with it. He felt Lance's cock against him, hard and leaking. Without breaking the hot kiss, he reached over with one hand and opened the drawer, got the oil and a condom and put that hand behind Lance's back, letting him feel them against him.

Lance pulled back and looked down at him. Keen smiled up and said, "How do you want me?"

"Truth?" Lance asked, like he had before.

"Of course, truth," he answered as he had previously.

"I want you to bend over the side of the bed, and I want to plough you until you're shaking for me." Lance couldn't help the blush, but he said what he wanted.

"God, you are one sexy fuck, aren't you?" Keen moved to slide over to the side of the bed, wanting to set it up the way Lance wanted it. He stood, leaning to pull Lance up to stand beside him. He took him in his arms and rubbed his nose in Lance's neck, licking and sucking, holding him tight.

He stopped quickly, though, not wanting to take away from what Lance wanted. He handed the items to Lance and turned, bending over the bed, presenting him with his ass, spreading his legs, and pushing back, open, vulnerable and trusting. It was sexy as hell.

Lance made short work of getting himself ready then bent to slide his tongue along the crack of Keen's ass again. Keen yelped, not expecting the soft wet caress. He was no fool. He reached back and spread his cheeks, making it easier for Lance to continue. Lance pushed his tongue inside him again, and Keen groaned. He was already so sensitised there. He couldn't help the groans pouring forth from him. But he wanted more.

"Please, Lance, fuck me," he muttered, turning to see behind him. Lance pulled up to look into his face, the desire there for him to see. He took more oil, pushing two then three, fingers inside Keen's welcoming body and moving them around, getting him prepared.

"Yes!" Keen screamed into the bed covers as Lance put his cock at his entrance and rammed home in one long, smooth move. Keen tried to be quiet, tried hard. Lance gave him no quarter. He set about plunging into him over and over, taking him hard and deep. Keen braced himself against the bed and pushed back, taking more, wanting more.

Lance held his hips and didn't slow down at all. He moved, pushing downward and was rewarded with another short scream as he managed to hit Keen's gland, sending him into another hard orgasm.

Keen felt Lance's climax coming. He revelled in Lance's yell, feeling the cum bursting out of him, filling the condom in long spurts. Lance slowed down, never letting go of Keen, who was sprawled across the bed, breathing hard but still pushing back to take him in with each thrust. He slowly eased out, standing for a second, holding on to Keen to steady himself.

Sex with Lance was… Keen wasn't sure he could think of a word strong enough to describe the wonder of it, the intensity. He gave up, taking Lance into his arms.

"I know we have to order supper and see about Phoebe, but can we lie down just for a few minutes?" Lance asked. Keen knew they both needed to wind down, and he was pleased that Lance wanted to do it in his arms.

"Oh, yeah. That is definitely in order." He climbed up on the bed, feeling it move as Lance followed him. They turned to each other and reached out, settling onto the bed and into each other's arms. It was just what they needed.

They rested together for a few minutes then got up to take a quick shower together.

While moving the soft soapy sponge over Lance, Keen noticed that Lance was quiet and slow all of a sudden. He was learning his lover's tells like a seasoned poker player. Something was bothering him. After their wonderful afternoon, Keen had to wonder.

"What is it, Lance? Why so quiet?" Keen sluiced the water down Lance's back and buttocks, washing away the fragrant soap but keeping his eyes on Lance to see his reaction to the question.

"I'm an idiot, borrowing trouble. I just keep thinking life is going to kick us in the face. I feel like it's too good, too soon. Can we be this happy? I don't think I've ever really been *un*happy, but everything is, like, *so* wonderful, I'm waiting for the other shoe to drop."

"Shh... It's okay. Don't feel that way. You deserve to be this happy. You're a great person. You're a good brother, a great friend and a fabulous lover. Don't second guess your happiness. Maybe you were meant to be this happy. You ever think of it that way, that it was just your fate to be this gloriously happy?" Keen tried to tease him out of the mood, but he also meant just what he was saying.

"You're right. I told you I was being an idiot. I feel silly. We're good together, and we're doing a good thing with Miss Phoebe. I shouldn't question it, just enjoy it. Here, kiss me better. You know you can." Lance grinned as he said it.

Taking Lance's face between his hands, Keen looked at him and said, "Don't worry. Life will throw something at us. It always does. No one gets through without pain or sorrow or even catastrophe. It's how you deal with it, and who you have to help you, that makes all the difference in the world. Now, come here, I think a kiss was requested." Keen paused a second. "Just one?"

"Well, when you put it that wa—mmph—" Lance opened for Keen's tongue and the shower took a little longer than they'd planned.

Keen went out to check on Phoebe while Lance looked through the list of take-out places. They both wanted pizza and Phoebe wanted a salad, she said, as she walked into the kitchen. They ate together in the living room, watching television then they all went to bed early, ready for the big day tomorrow.

Chapter Nine

Keen led Phoebe into the house and eased her down onto the sofa. She was still sputtering and gasping. He wasn't worried that she was having a heart attack or anything. She was in absolute shock. He was so tickled for her. He couldn't wait to tell Lance and the others.

"Keen, honey, are you sure he wasn't just pulling my leg? You didn't tell him to say all that, did you? He couldn't really mean that I would make that much money on the books now. It's just not... I can't take it all in." Her eyes literally looked as if they had stars in them.

"I can't think of anyone who deserves it more, and no, I didn't tell him to say anything. I knew he loved your work and am not surprised he toiled so hard to get a deal for you. Ron's a good guy. I'm a little surprised it's all happening so soon. Are you ready for the big day? Next Saturday is pretty soon. How about a shopping trip with Sandy for a new dress for the party-reception thing they're throwing for you?"

Phoebe's eyes got even wider and brighter. "Oh, give me a minute. I still can't believe it. It's all so wonderful. Yes, I'd love to go shopping for something new. I'll even be able to pay you back soon."

Keen smiled at her excitement. "Not a chance. This is on me. I'd love to buy you a beautiful dress for your special night. You'll need two nice outfits, one for the activities that day and one for the reception that night. I'll leave that to you and Sandy."

He was already looking forward to running by and picking up Lance for lunch and telling him everything about the fabulous deal Ron had worked out for Phoebe. She would be a rich old lady before long. Keen was thrilled for her and knew Lance would be, too.

Phoebe had asked to come home and spend the afternoon just resting and thinking about all that had happened.

"Are you sure you're okay? You don't need anything? I'm not sure I should leave you. You're pretty hyped up." Keen tried not to let on that he was worried about her health.

"Go on and get Lance. You know you're dying to see him and tell him how your plan worked so well. I'm fine. I just need to sit and think about everything. You've changed my life, Keen, you and Lance and Sandy and Kale. You've made me so unbelievably happy. Go now and let me take it all in." Miss Phoebe made a production out of sweeping her legs up onto the couch and reclining back, one hand over her head like a dramatically-posing movie star from the fifties.

Keen laughed and shook his head. She was a card. "I think we'll go out tonight and celebrate with a good dinner. Put on your best duds, darlin'. No one's cooking or cleaning up tonight. It's a special occasion. I'll see you a little later this afternoon. I'm happy for you, sweetie."

He slipped over and told Kale the news and got his promise to let Sandy know about this morning and the plans for the evening. They called one of the best restaurants in town and reserved a table for later that night. Then he headed out to pick up his man for lunch.

He deliberately didn't call ahead. He wanted to tell Lance in person, and he liked to walk in and catch Lance working. He loved watching him in action. The man was just poetry in motion, absolutely amazing. And *his*. He smiled as he saw Lance alone on the mat. There were no classes right now, so he was just practicing and he looked *good*.

Keen watched a few more minutes then began to applaud. Lance stopped and turned to him.

"Hey! You're here. How long…oh! How'd it go? Tell me! Come on!" Lance was obviously anxious to hear about how things went for Phoebe. He had shown in many ways that he'd come to love the old lady like a grandmother.

"Want to come with me for lunch? I've got take-out in the truck, an empty office and news to share. How long do you have?" Keen asked his eager lover, who bounced as he waited for news.

"Almost two hours before my next class. This is a slow day. Tomorrow is a lot busier. Come on, I can't wait. Tell me something."

"It's better than we even hoped. How's that? Now, come on." Keen grabbed his hand, only dropping it as they got out the door.

It was a quick trip to Keen's office, and Lance laughed when he saw the desk had been cleared again. Keen put down the fast food and pulled him into his arms.

"Door?" asked Keen

"Locked," Lance shot back.

"Excellent, come here." Keen kissed the living daylights out of him. Lance didn't seem to mind. He gave back as good as he got. They'd enjoy a bit of dessert before the meal. Soon, breathing was laboured and hands were wandering.

"Mmph…hey…baby," Keen finally managed to say.

"Mmm…" Lance didn't seem quite ready to stop what he was doing just yet.

Keen pulled away, eventually, and said, "God, you're sexy."

"*Me?* You." Lance finally put his face into Keen's neck and just breathed.

"Okay, we're both sexy as hell. Come on, let's eat and I'll tell you about the meeting this morning and the plans for tonight."

"Ooh. Sounds good. Tell all."

They divided up the meal, sat close and talked. Keen told him the great deal Ron had worked out for Phoebe and how much they expected her to make from it. Lance's eyes were huge. Keen smiled and reached to touch his nose in a small caress. He was so sweet and excited for their friend.

"Wow. That is too cool."

"Hey, it was your idea. You got it all started with your 'I have an idea'." Keen mimicked Lance's hesitant voice from that night the ideas had flown around.

Lance blushed, looking happy, clearly thinking of how he had helped set this in motion.

"So, what's tonight?"

"We're going to one of the best places in town for a celebration dinner with Phoebe and the others. Dress up time. You got dress-up clothes?"

"Uh. No. Looks like I need to shop a little. Where do you suggest?"

"I'll take you when you get off this afternoon, and we'll both get some new stuff. I'm sending Sandy and Phoebe out to get new dresses for the big day and night's activities next Saturday."

"I've got the money for it, not a problem. I'd love to have you help me pick out some stuff, though. You've got good instincts. You always look great."

"No problem. See you about…what…four-thirty?"

They agreed that Keen would pick Lance up and they'd shop quickly and be ready to take the others out to dinner.

* * * *

They had a wonderful celebration dinner filled with laughter and delight in the success of their plans. Everyone was thrilled with the news from the meeting and strategies for the launch of the campaign to market Phoebe's books again and the reception afterward. Two weeks after that there would be an auction, led by Ron's company, for the originals. They discussed back and forth whether it would be better to auction them singly or as a group.

Keen's argument was that singly they would make nine people happy whereas if they went as a group only one person would be thrilled. He believed in sharing the joy.

"But you have copies of all of them, so you can say that," Kale said.

"Yes, but I had all her books already. I guarantee whoever buys these at auction will, too. I think we'd get more if we went individually."

"Well, with all that dear man said I would maybe get from reselling the books, I'm not so worried about getting more, but I like your idea of more people being happy to have them," Phoebe chimed in.

"Then that answers that. You get the deciding vote," Keen said.

"I still think you should keep them if you'd like them." She tried one more time to get him to accept them.

"No way. I've got you, my copies and my autographs. I'm one happy man." His bright smile left her in no doubt.

"I need you to do me a favour, fairly soon, if you don't mind," Phoebe said, looking at Keen.

"Anything. Just ask."

"I'd like to meet with a lawyer and arrange for what happens to anything that comes in after I leave this world. I have some definite ideas on that. It wasn't long ago that I thought there'd be…not even enough to bury me. Now I have to figure out what to do with what is a…a fortune to me." She shook her head again at the wonder of it all.

"Sure. I'd be glad to. My lawyer is a lady named Angela Henderson. She's great. If you'd like, I'll get in touch with her tomorrow and set something up for you."

"That would be fine. You're always so very helpful to me."

"It's easy when you care for someone."

* * * *

Two months later

"I miss her."

"Me, too. I got used to having her around. She really didn't cramp our style like she claimed. She was *fun* to be with. Reckon she's happy over there?" Keen asked, voicing what he'd been wondering for a while now.

"We could go see her. Not call ahead but show up and see if we think she's happier there. If not, what do you think about…?"

"Asking her to come back here?" Keen finished for him, knowing Lance had really missed having Phoebe around in the last weeks.

Phoebe had moved into an assisted living residence about ten minutes from their house a couple of weeks ago. She told them on the phone that she loved it there. They both doubted it. She was with a lot of people, but not with the people who loved her.

"You have to think about this seriously, Lance. This is your home. If we can talk her into coming back and living here, she'll also be dying here." He paused a second at the look of horror on Lance's face. "That sounds harsh, but she's almost ninety-one. While she's healthy now, she doesn't have a whole lot longer to live. Can you handle it when she's older, frail, sick and then gone? It won't be easy. That might just be the other shoe you've been waiting for to drop."

Keen had to be responsible for all their sakes. He had to admit he had been thinking the same things. He'd love to go and offer Phoebe a home with them until the end. It felt right.

"You're right. It would be hard," Lance agreed, then went on, "but not as hard as if we just heard about her dying in a phone call from there. Here she would be happy and know that everyone around her cared about her. Don't think I won't be really hurt when she's gone, but I'd be happier if she was with us until she had to go, ya know?"

Keen got up and walked around, thinking it over as he paced. "Yeah, I know. I've been thinking about it. Here she's got all that money and can do what she wants, but she's still basically alone. If she were suffering from dementia or something I could see her needing to be there, but she just went so we could…what…walk around the house naked? I think we're on the same page here. Wanna see what Sandy and Kale think?"

Maybe fresh perspectives might help them make that decision…and help them convince Phoebe to come back home.

Lance hopped up and they headed next door where they knew Sandy was home today. Kale had a few more days leave then he'd be back in Cincinnati and Sandy, Keen knew, would be devastated. But, so far, Kale hadn't made any noises about making the two of them permanent. Keen knew Kale had feelings for Sandy, feelings that were definitely returned.

That was their business. Still, he really wished things would work out for them.

* * * *

Keen and Lance were on a mission. They drove to the place where Phoebe was living now and instead of parking in the front, they decided to park in the back and walk around to the front. Keen was scoping out the place, checking on things, making sure it was as good a place as they'd originally thought. Plus, he was looking for ammo to use in his argument about taking her back home with them. If they could find something wrong with the place…

It was honestly as if she were a family member and he had to be sure she was happy and safe and really enjoying herself in her new digs. Keen was looking around when Lance reached to touch his arm. He stopped walking immediately and glanced questioningly at Lance.

Lance put his finger to his lips and pointed. Keen's eyes nearly bugged out of his head and his mouth gaped open. His first instinct was to yell, "What in the holy hell are you doing?" but he was afraid that would startle the man who balanced precariously on the windowsill of one of the rooms. There was no ladder, and a fall probably wouldn't kill him, but injury was certainly possible. How'd he even get up there? What could he possibly be doing?

Keen glanced back to Lance and, as usual, it was obvious the man had a plan. He motioned for Keen to follow quietly, and in seconds, they stood below the man who now tried to open the window with one hand while hanging on with the other.

With a quick glance at Lance, Keen spoke quietly, "I know there's going to be a really good reason why you're breaking in here." Before he could go on, the man grunted and turned, losing his balance and falling. Keen and Lance both reached out and managed to break his fall enough for him to escape injury, but they held on tight when he tried to cut and run.

"Start talking," Keen demanded.

"Why should I? You don't look like a cop to me," the man spat out and jerked his arm, trying to get away from them.

"Lance," Keen started.

"On it," Lance replied and finished dialling 9-1-1 for the police and started talking.

The man turned quickly and swung his right arm around trying to get a good hit against Lance. Lance was much too agile and quick for that. He ducked and took the man's arm and twisted it up behind his back.

Keen held on more tightly now, giving the man no chance for a repeat attempt at hurting either of them or getting away.

"Hey! Let me go. Come on, man," the man said, trying now for pleading instead of belligerence.

"Nope, not happening. You can explain to the nice officer who comes to take you away. See, I just couldn't think of a good reason for you to be breaking into a window at this place. Can't be a legal reason, so I'm assuming you were up to no good."

"Who're you, anyway? What business is it of yours?" the man, resigned to his fate, was just angry now.

"I think that falls under none of *your* business," Keen told him as they heard sirens in the distance.

Lance was curious. "What were you doing trying to break in the window at a place like this?"

"Heard there was a rich old lady here. She don't need it. I was gonna — get away from me, you. Let go, the cops are here. You better not hurt me or…I'll…"

Lucky for him, the cops were there. He didn't get the beating both Lance and Keen were ready to dispense. Had he been trying to get in to Phoebe? Keen thought he'd make sure.

"What rich old lady?"

Lance had walked up to meet the officers as they'd gotten out of the car and was telling them what he and Keen had caught the man doing.

"Answer me, what lady are you talking about?"

"Some old broad who wrote a bunch of porn books, and now she's got all this money. She's got no need of it and don't deserve it neither. Bunch of queer trash." This coming from a man willing to steal from said 'old broad'. Speaking of trash...

Keen seethed. This thief was talking about Phoebe! He'd known it. For some reason, he'd known it when he'd seen the man. He'd had a strong feeling of foreboding.

He looked over as Lance and the officers came up. Keen couldn't believe it was Officer Ragan again. How big of an area did this man cover?

"You guys again? What's going on? You thinking of joining the force? What is it with you two?"

Keen managed a chuckle and said, "In this case, right place, right time. This piece of shit was trying to break into a ninety-year-old woman's room to steal from her. I hope you have a special place for crap like this." It would be a while before Keen got over his anger at the man

The director of the complex was contacted, and he met with the policemen, Keen, and Lance. It wasn't long before the squad car was leaving with the would-be thief inside. Keen told Lance what he'd learned about the man's plan. Lance had the expected reaction.

"*That* does it. She needs to come home," he said, looking at Keen for his agreement.

"Yeah, that's kind of what I was thinking," Keen admitted.

When they finally got inside, they found Phoebe sitting in a large chair as if she'd been waiting for them. She looked so tiny in that big chair...sort of out of place. Keen smiled as Lance hurried over to her and drew her up for a hug. Keen didn't know who this plan would help most, Lance or Phoebe.

"Boys! What's going on?" she asked against Lance's chest. "What's all the excitement? Oh, I'm so happy to see you!" She beamed as she switched to Keen's arms now.

"Um, the police caught a guy outside. No big deal," Keen glossed it over then said, "Phoebe, we have a problem."

"What is it, hon? Can I help? I mean, I figure, since you're here, it has something to do with me. Was there a mistake about all that money? I knew it was too good to be true..." She looked worried as she looked back and forth between them.

"No, sweetheart, the money's fine. It's all there, with more coming," Keen assured her.

"Then what...?" She looked puzzled.

Lance was his usual blunt self.

"We want you to come home and live with us again." He blushed as he finished, but didn't back down.

"Oh. Oh! Lance, honey, you don't mean that. You all just got your home back to yourselves. I would just..."

"You didn't like living with us?" Lance asked, sincere in his concern. "Did we bother you?"

"Oh, no, honey. Y'all were wonderful. I loved being with you both. You're such good men and so sweet to me. You're my knights, remember? I just couldn't intrude." Phoebe's eyes were huge as if she couldn't take it all in.

"Phoebe, we talked about it and we agreed," Keen said quietly. "It's what we'd both like. We liked having you with us. We enjoy your company. We all have our own areas and when we want to be apart, it's no problem. We love you. We want you with us. This isn't just a whim. We both want you to come home. Will you think about it, seriously?" Keen finished, looking hopeful. His voice was laced with sincerity. He couldn't help smiling as her eyes widened at his words.

She looked at them with tears welled up in her eyes, threatening to spill over.

"You're serious. I...I don't know what to say." Phoebe just sat right back down in that big chair and both hands went up to her face in the gesture they both recognised as one she used when she was overwhelmed...or delighted.

"Have you all thought this through? I mean, it would have to be an imposition. You don't need an old woman around when you want to be together...or feel like you have to take me with you when you go somewhere...or..." She trailed off as they both shook their heads at her.

"You lived with us for over a month, and we didn't take you everywhere, just when it was what we all wanted. You need your time alone and so do we. We realised that. We didn't lack for any time alone together. We managed to do all that we wanted with you somewhere else in the house or over at Sandy's or...come on, you know how it was." Keen looked at her, wanting her to admit that it had worked out well for all of them.

"Lance, honey," she said, looking closely at him, "are you sure you want an old lady cramping your style like that...all the time?"

"Yes, ma'am. I'm sure. I liked having you there with us. You made it seem like a family. You made our home complete," Lance admitted, really blushing now at sounding so...sweet.

"That has to be the nicest thing anyone has said to me in...longer than I can remember. You're both sure?" It was as if she almost couldn't let herself believe it. "I was so happy with you all when I lived in the house. I'm okay here. This place is really nice and they try to make us feel like we're all important, but…it's not the same…as family." Tears rolled down her cheeks as she finished.

"Ah now, none of that. We don't want to make you cry. We just want you to come back with us, if you're sure it would make you happy, too." Keen put his hands out and smoothed the tears from her cheeks then patted her shoulder.

Phoebe reached into the pocket of her slacks suit, got out a tissue and cleaned up then said, "What are we waiting for? I want to go home." All three smiled hugely as they helped her up and went to gather her things and talk to the manager of the facility.

Chapter Ten

It was a happy group that settled into the large corner booth at one of the big steakhouses that stayed open really late on the weekends. The place was nearly empty. Despite the late hour, Phoebe was as loud and boisterous as the rest of them. They were celebrating tonight. Sandy, Kale, Phoebe, Keen, and Lance.

"I'm so proud of you, I can't contain it," Sandy said, touching Lance on the arm, her eyes shining with pride. "You should have brought that big-ass trophy in with you so everyone would know how good you are."

"I don't think so. Besides," he smiled back at her, "they can all hear you. Will you tone it down?" Actually, the self-deprecation was real. Keen had learned that Lance didn't really like the spotlight on himself too much. But tonight he deserved accolades.

Keen leant over to Lance's ear and whispered something, causing a deep blush to spread from Lance's neck to his hairline.

"Kee—eeen!" he said, embarrassed, but pleased, too, they could all tell.

"Oh, Kee, I don't want to know," Kale teased and Sandy ducked her head against Kale's shoulder as if she were embarrassed. Like there was anything that would embarrass her! Phoebe just smiled at them.

"So, um…you all liked the exhibition, huh? All of it, I mean. Hammer was awesome, wasn't he? The whole group was great. We took most of the trophies in all the events we entered." His pride was showing as he talked and they all agreed that the event was wonderful and that his dojo was the obvious winner. Hammer was indeed awesome. But it was Lance they were celebrating tonight.

The waitress came and took orders all around and Phoebe demanded the right to get the cheque. They let her as it seemed so important to her and they knew she could well afford it now.

Conversation flowed around the table as they all ate heartily and talked about the exhibition and some of Hammer's plans, like expansion and maybe using Lance as manager of the present dojo as Hammer went to open the new one. That was a big jump after such a short time. Not that Lance wasn't capable of doing a great job. Keen had no doubts about Lance's abilities.

"Sandy and I have something to tell you all." This came from Kale.

It just hung there in a moment of silence. They all looked over at the couple and a revelation wasn't necessary. There was dawning comprehension on all three faces as they looked at the couple who could barely contain their happiness.

"No way!" said Keen.

"Way!" said Kale.

"Cool!" chimed in Lance.

"Oh, wonderful!" came from Phoebe.

"Why didn't you tell us?" Keen demanded.

"We just did, you goof," Sandy said and got up to come over and hug Keen who'd gotten up to meet her. He held her tight to him and said into her ear, "I'm so happy for you, darling."

"Hey, you hittin' on my girl?" Kale asked, laughing, "come on over here, Lance, I'm gonna…"

"You're gonna, my ass. Hands off, Ka." Keen let Sandy go and sat back down, mock glaring at his brother.

"Right back at ya, Kee, don't be snuggling up to my future wife like that."

"Oh, boys, you are both such wonderful idiots. I think each of you has the partner of your dreams. I'm so happy for all of you." Phoebe settled the group down.

"Phoebe, will you help me plan my wedding?" Sandy asked, seriously.

"Oh, I'd love to help you, if you think you want an old lady's ideas."

"Definitely. I'd love you to be in it, too."

"Oh, come on, you can't be serious," Phoebe looked at Sandy with an incredulous expression. "I'm old as the hills. You need…"

"I need someone I love to be with me up there. We'll see if Mom and Angelo can come for it." Sandy's face was lit from within as she talked about her initial plans. "I know we want both Keen and Lance in it. I think we'd like it to be in the back yard, then we can use both houses for the reception and party. We're not looking for big and fancy. We just want family and loved ones. What do you all think?" She looked at the three of them, as if she thought they might have a problem with anything she wanted.

"Anything you want, anywhere you want, we'll do whatever makes you happy," Keen put in. Lance nodded his agreement. Phoebe just smiled with tears in her eyes as she looked at her family.

"So, uh…where will you all live?" Keen asked, hating the thought of them moving to Cincinnati.

"Oh, didn't I tell you?" Kale had a shit-eating grin on his face that made Keen want to come right across the table at him.

"No, you didn't tell me. What are you grinnin' at, Ka?"

"I've been transferred to the Nashville Police Department. My captain arranged it after I called to resign from up there." Kale's hand absently massaged the back of Sandy's neck as he talked to the group. "He went on about losing a good man and what was I going to do. I told him I'd like to get on down here and he said he'd get back to me. Evidently, he went to school with someone here and next thing you know, I'm in."

He sat up straighter and looked over at Keen with a twinkle in his eyes. "We're staying right where we are now, right beside you. Think you can stand it?" Kale smiled as he asked the question. He knew the answer. They all did. It was perfect.

"That's great, Kale." Keen said, thrilled that he was going to be close to his brother. Being with him a lot recently had made him realise how much he had missed him. God, he was going to be living with his lover and their great friend, Phoebe, next door to his best friend and his brother. Perfect.

Keen jumped as he felt Lance's hand on his thigh, squeezing tight. He looked over. That wasn't a caress. It hurt.

Lance's gaze was riveted to the front of the restaurant where the reservation desk was located. Keen looked over and put his hand down on top of Lance's to let him know he was aware that Lance wanted something from him. He watched a second to see what was going on out there.

Well, hell. The young girl at the hostess desk was standing, mouth agape, as a young man pointed a gun at her and talked rapidly. She shook her head and he waved the gun again and she gasped. He raised his hand as if to hit her, probably to quiet her. She shrank back and he growled something.

Keen looked at Kale and said, "There's a man with a gun, harassing the hostess. She's freaked and he's about to lose it."

Kale looked at Sandy and said, "You and Phoebe lie down in the seat and stay down until one of us tells you to move. Promise...right now." He knew she would want to try to help, but she had to protect Phoebe right now.

She nodded and within the big booth the two of them slid apart and down they went with their heads together. They curled their legs up onto the bench seat and looked like they were ready for a nap.

Keen glanced over at Lance and before he could say anything, he saw that Lance had his cell phone out and had already dialled 9-1-1. "On it," he said.

Keen spared just a second to be proud of Lance's quickness and steadiness.

He looked at Kale and raised a brow.

"Don't think about it. You let the locals handle it, Keen." Kale warned him. He had eased around so he could try to get a glimpse of what was happening. Keen could tell that Kale was dying to get his absent gun and go handle the situation. It was just who he was.

"Forget it. We s'posed to just watch him shoot her? He's getting more and more upset while we sit here and argue," Keen was already getting to his feet.

It was a good thing that the lateness of the hour made for a nearly empty place. There was one young couple further back, who remained clueless as they had eyes only for each other.

The next things that happened were like a kaleidoscope. All of it jumbled together, one right after the other, making a mixed picture.

Lance cut right and low, heading for the other couple where he spoke quickly to the guy, who grabbed his girl and headed for the corner, staying down. He covered her with his body and waited for help to arrive.

Keen had already headed for the front so Kale had no choice but to follow his lead, hoping no one got shot. As they neared the front they could hear the hostess crying and begging the man not to shoot her and swearing that she had no way of getting to any money. The man was strung out on something. He wasn't totally coherent as he waved the gun about, moved his weight from foot to foot, and got louder in his demands. He wasn't very big, with long stringy blond hair that kept getting in his wild-looking eyes.

Keen wondered where the management was, not sure whether he wanted someone else to show up or if that would just cause more of a problem. He and Kale were about to make it a little crowded out there.

"If we don't get shot, I'm gonna kick your ass!" Kale promised, quietly.

"Like you could stand to do nothing. Just follow along. We can't watch something like this happen and not do anything," Keen whispered and then in a loud voice, he yelled at Kale and pushed him, making him lurch towards the front, pretty close to the hostess's podium.

Both the girl and the gun-wielding man turned at this interruption, she with hope in her eyes and he with consternation.

"Back off, asshole," Kale shouted. Good man.

"I told you to lay off," Keen said, pushing him again, this time right into the girl. Kale caught her around the waist and took her down, twisting so she'd land on him, not the other way around.

"Now look what you did, idiot," Kale yelled over her. He turned then to put her below him, covering her.

Keen didn't even look at Kale, but turned to the man, acting as if he didn't even see the gun.

"Do you believe this shit?" He asked the man, as if he were trying to get the man to side with him against Kale. The man was momentarily nonplussed, looking from Keen to Kale who was now covering the girl.

From behind Keen, Lance rushed up and said, "Dude, the cops!" and pointed out the side window to the right. The man just had to glance that way. Lance's leg flew up like a flash and the gun went spinning up into the air. Lance turned and used the other leg to sweep the man's feet out from under him. Keen dropped down and forced him onto his stomach. Lance jumped over him and made a grab for the gun before it hit the floor, afraid it might go off and hit someone.

Kale hopped up from the girl, helping her up. Lance handed him the gun, took the girl and headed away from the scene. He helped her to a seat at one of the first tables and eased her down.

"You're okay, hon. You did good. Can you get a manager or someone out here now?" Lance wanted to give her something productive to do in an effort to ward off hysteria.

Kale laid they gun down on the podium so he wouldn't be caught holding it when the police came in.

"You gonna be able to stay on him, keep him still, Keen?" Kale asked. He didn't think it would be a good idea to let the furious man upright. "Need help?"

"Got it. I'm good," Keen said, although it was a little like riding an alligator, an alligator with a really foul mouth.

Finally they heard sirens about the time, the girl, whose nametag identified her as Tina, brought the manager towards them.

"What the hell's going on here?" Manny asked. Keen and Lance looked at each other and nearly laughed out loud. Not another Manny!

"Your hostess, here, Tina, just did a great job of helping us subdue this man. He was waving a gun around and wanted, what Tina?" Kale said, looking over at her.

"He...he wanted money, but I kept telling him I didn't have any up here. He just kept getting madder and madder." She looked between the three men who'd save her and said, "Thanks, guys."

Before they could answer her, the doors burst open and police officers, guns drawn, were there, yelling and making a great show of force.

"Guys, guys," Kale said, using his no nonsense police voice. "Relax. The situation is under control. I think my brother might like a couple of you to relieve him of his current ride, though. This man came in with a gun, demanding money. Uh, the gun's right there," he pointed to the podium.

"So who're you all?" one of the officers asked, putting away his gun while the other two took over the now-prisoner.

"Oh, I can answer that, Bobby. I've met at least two of these characters before, more than once. You guys are unbelievable, always in the thick of things. And tell me, I'm not seeing double!" Officer Ragan said, looking at Kale and rolling his eyes.

"Just trying to help, sir. I'm Kale Thomas, a fellow officer from Cincinnati. I'll be transferring down here really soon, and —"

He was interrupted by the officer, "And you thought it would be a good way to work your way in by jumping in and taking over in a situation where innocent people could get killed? That was not smart, Thomas, and I'll be —"

"Hey," Keen broke in. "Back off, it was *my* idea. Kale was against it from the beginning. He wanted to wait for you all. But I was *not* gonna let *him*," he pointed to the prisoner, "shoot her. He was *this* close," he showed how close with his thumb and finger, leaving little space between.

"He couldn't stop you, huh? Why doesn't that surprise me?" the officer said, shaking his head.

"Don't even think about trying to blame Kale for this. I forced it. I know it was dangerous, but I couldn't sit and do nothing." Keen looked at the officer and said, spreading his hands and shrugging, "It's not like when she told him she didn't have access to any money he just went away saying, 'Okay, no problem, thanks, ma'am.' You see him. Can't you tell he's freaked on something?"

Next up was the young couple, full of praise and wonder at the way the three men had handled the volatile situation. The young man told how Lance had warned them to stay down and they had huddled near where Phoebe and Sandy were lying in the booth. Actually he sort of helped the situation with his words.

"They were like a team you see on TV. They weren't being big show offs, ya know?" he said, looking right into the cop's eyes. "They made sure that girl was okay first and then worked together to get the man down. They're heroes for sure." He ducked his head and admitted, "I...uh...I saw it all. I was supposed to be keeping down. They told me to, but I leaned out far enough to watch."

"Kale!" Sandy ran up and grabbed him and held tight, then moved to Keen for a quick hug and then on to Lance for another. Phoebe did the same, but she started with Keen, then Lance, then Kale. The policeman looked on, bewildered.

"Ma'am, what...who...?" His momentary incoherence nearly made her smile, but she broke in.

"Fiancé, best friend, brother." She answered pointing respectively.

"Uh-huh," he said, watching as the other two officers cuffed the man and read him his rights. He motioned them on out to the car and he turned back, this time looking at Phoebe.

"Hey, aren't you the one that...?" Officer Ragan shook his head. Maybe he thought he was losing it himself, seeing the same people over and over.

"Uh, this is my family," Phoebe said, simply.

"Okay. Well, whatever. I'm gonna need some of your time, men. Can you come down to the station with us? We need to get this processed."

Sandy spoke up, "I'll take Phoebe home in my car and you all can go do manly things with the nice officer. We'll be waiting for you at Keen's house."

"Great," Kale answered, "you're gonna make a great cop's wife." He dropped a quick kiss on her lips and hugged her tight for a minute.

Keen and Lance each hugged Phoebe and told her to go on to bed when she got home and they'd tell her everything about it tomorrow morning.

"Bull, I'll be waiting up with coffee and cinnamon rolls when you all get home later," she said, her chin up and her arms crossed.

"Wicked!" Lance said, grabbing her again and hugging her quickly.

* * * *

It was a *tired* group that sat down nearly two hours later at Keen's house for coffee and Phoebe's fabulous cinnamon rolls.

The ladies had spent the time getting things ready for the men to come in and relax. They both said they were proud of their guys and were eager to pamper them a little. They'd been talking quietly for quite a while when they heard the men returning.

Sandy pushed the button starting the coffee and Phoebe was just taking the second pan of rolls out of the oven when the men filed in. The kitchen smelled wonderful and was just what the returning heroes needed to unwind.

"Oh my God, Phoebe, you're the best! That smell is...mmm, forget the smell," Lance said, grabbing one from the plate on the counter and putting near half of it in his mouth, "thasss soooooo goooooom" he swallowed, and corrected himself "….uh good." He devoured the rest of it and ran his finger across his chin to catch some of the glaze. He heard a sound and looked over. Keen was watching him.

Keen wanted to go right over and lick that sweetness right off Lance's face. He was sure the desire was evident in his eyes. He shared a look of promise with Lance.

The guys answered questions for a while as everyone got what they needed and sat around the table enjoying the treats the ladies had prepared.

Kale had spent some time with the officers after it was made clear he was not hot-dogging at the restaurant. His had been the voice of reason, and the officers finally admitted the situation was handled as well as could be given the circumstances. They had to bring up, though, that they didn't recommend civilians taking on the bad guys as a rule. That had gotten them into a discussion of the numerous times that Keen and Lance had stepped in and helped out in situations. They were now *officially* known as The Chaos Magnets. Great.

Eventually Kale and Sandy headed next door after getting hugs and congratulations from the other three. Phoebe headed to her room, finally admitting she was ready for bed. That left Keen and Lance.

They quickly cleared the mess and cleaned up. As Lance turned off the kitchen light and started out the door towards their room, Keen grabbed his hand and pulled him back into the darkened kitchen. From the small glow of the clock on the microwave Keen could see the question on Lance's face. He pulled him into his arms and squeezed hard.

"Mmph," Lance grunted as his ribs nearly cracked. "Keen…baby?"

Keen put his face into Lance's neck and inhaled deeply and moved his hands hard over Lance's back, keeping Lance tight against him.

"I love you."

"I know you do. I love you, too." Lance tried to raise his head up but Keen put his hand up and held it to his shoulder. He needed this hug, this tightness. He needed to hold and be held.

Lance caught on quick and gave him back the same strong embrace. He held on to Keen and waited to see what his man needed from him.

"You scare me sometimes…" Keen started.

"Me? What…you mean to*night*…with the guy? You're the one who held him down. Lord, he had to have been high on something. He was *strong*." Lance said, giving Keen credit. "You started it all, helped save the girl. I'm so proud of you." Lance rubbed his face on Keen's shoulder turning it into his neck and kissing him there.

"Don't get me wrong," Keen began huskily, "I know you can take care of yourself…and God knows you're good with your feet, but it just finally hit me that things could have gone really wrong tonight. I could have lost you. Scared me for a minute," he added, ruefully.

"I know, same here. Somehow when we're together and something bad like that comes up, we just seem to work well as a team and get things done." Lance took a deep breath before he admitted, "I had the same kind of …sort of anxiety attack earlier when you were talking to one of the guys. You just didn't see it. I feel the same way. It hit me how it could have gone down." Lance shuddered against Keen. "I can't lose you, Keen. Out of the question. You hear?" He tightened his arms around Keen now.

"Uh, yeah. That's kind of what this is all about. Gotta let you know how very much you mean to me and how I can't do without you and…ground covered…wanna just shut me up here?" Keen turned his head and met Lance's advancing mouth and they shared a hard bruising kiss that *almost* got the edge off both of them.

Keen couldn't seem to let go. They were still plastered together head to toe, as if to make sure nothing could part them. The heat and strength of that kiss went a long way towards easing their minds and calming their sudden fears. Keen knew it filled a need they both seemed to have. Since they couldn't actually crawl right into each other's skin and take up residence, this closeness would have to do for right now.

As one, they turned and headed down the hall to the bedroom. Keen led Lance into the bathroom and leant in to start the shower, getting it just right. He turned and started helping Lance get naked. He followed suit and they stepped in together.

They soaped and slid and rubbed and smoothed, shampooed and cleansed and tasted and sighed, dried and massaged and caressed and loved. When they made it to the bed, both were tired and happy and strangely not so much horny as needy. By mutual unspoken consent they settled into the middle of the bed, wrapped as closely around each other as it was possible to get and then fell asleep, breathing each other's air, hearts pounding together.

Chapter Eleven

Keen had decided to recreate a scene from book number seven. He happened to know that was the one Lance would read next. Keen smiled, thinking about how Lance had been devouring the books. They often talked about characters in them and things that had happened to the couples as they struggled to make a life together. Keen couldn't count the times Lance had shook his head in awe thinking about how Phoebe had written the love scenes in them.

With Phoebe's help, Keen had the night planned out to his satisfaction. When Lance got home there would be a meal ready for him. Phoebe was spending the night at Sandy's. She had enjoyed helping him set up the things he needed for tonight.

For Keen, there were no questions about what he was doing. He knew Lance was his love, his one love. He truly believed that Lance felt the same way. Lance had called his parents and explained he was staying here and had moved in with Keen, with Sandy's approval. That had helped.

They were living together, both considering this their home, but Keen wanted more. He wanted to make if official...not 'wedding' official but 'personal commitment' official. So, with a light heart, he'd worked all afternoon on his plans for tonight.

The meal was prepared and waiting for them, all Lance's and Keen's favourites. Keen could have just fixed Lance's favourites, but he was making a point here. They were equally important and went together well.

His gift for Lance was special. He had looked for a long time for just the right thing. He had gone to an artist Sandy had told him about and had the lyrics to *Time in a Bottle* by Jim Croce inscribed onto the outside of a large glass vase. It now sat in a beautiful box on the table ready for Lance to open. Inside the vase was a new watch – a really nice watch. The whole theme of the evening was time.

There was a card that read, "Lance, time means everything and nothing. It took very little time for me to know that I love you with all my heart. It isn't the *amount* of our time together, but the *quality* of that time. I want *time* with you, I will *make time* for you and I will love you for *all time*. Will you spend your remaining time with me? I want to travel with you, get to know more and more about you, and spend un*end*ing *time* making love with you. I love you. I want to hear you say those words to me. It's *time*. Actually, there's no *time* like the present. So, I am making a present of *time*. The watch is just a symbol of how much I want *time* with you. I am promising you all my love...and *my time*...Your lover, Keen."

They hadn't discussed things about the future. He didn't know how Lance would feel about a commitment ceremony. He wasn't sure he knew how he felt about it himself. That would be something they could discuss much later. Right now, he just wanted to let Lance know how seriously he was committed to the relationship they had.

He heard Lance coming in the door and went to meet him. The blinds were all drawn so it was darker than usual in the front room. He knew Lance would know something was up immediately. The candles spaced throughout the room were a dead giveaway. There were candles in the bedroom and bath just waiting to be lit and enjoyed. His heart sped up as did his steps as he saw Lance looking around the room, his eyes huge.

"Hey…" There was just that little bit of question in the word from Lance.

"Hey, yourself. Welcome home," Keen answered as he walked right into Lance's arms and took a kiss. Lance had dropped his duffel bag when he'd come in the door so his arms were free to wrap around Keen. He moaned as Keen's tongue pushed in and started moving. Didn't take him long to get into the game, though. He often told Keen that 'Kissing Keen' had quickly become one of his classes. Keen would answer that 'Loving Lance' was one of *his*.

Lance seemed to forget asking questions about the setting as they both got lost in the feelings of closeness and happiness. Finally, both silently admitting they had to stop and get a good breath, Lance put his face in Keen's neck and held on.

"Mmm… That was a really nice welcome home. I'm afraid I forgot some important date. Is something going on?" Lance finally got his question out.

"Maybe. I have the whole night planned just for us. Phoebe is at Sandy's for the night. We can make love all over the house if we want to, and I want to." He tightened his arms around Lance, giving him firm evidence of how much he wanted to. "We can eat first if you're hungry. I have something for you, too. We can do that first if you'd like that. Up to you. What do you want first?"

"No question. I want you." Lance moved back and forth from foot to foot, causing them to sway from side to side. "Something smells wonderful, I'm intrigued about what you have for me, but if you're asking what I want first, that's easy. I want you to come and shower with me and take me to bed then food then the surprise. That okay?" Now, he turned them so they were facing the hallway leading to the bedrooms.

Keen could tell Lance didn't want to mess up the order of things Keen had planned. Lance didn't know it yet, but whatever Lance wanted was what Keen had planned for them. Making his lover happy was his goal.

"My plan for you tonight is...anything you want. Let's go—no wait, you go get the shower running and I'll fix it so supper will be ready when *we're* ready for *it*. Scoot," he said, giving Lance a quick kiss then giving him a little push.

"Ooh, bossy, I think I like it...tonight." Lance laughed at the look on Keen's face. He scooted as told.

Keen got his magic done in the kitchen then followed a stunningly naked Lance into the shower.

"Oh, hello there. That was quick. C'mere," Lance said, pulling Keen into his arms. Keen stepped into the spray and the arms that were open to him.

They often shared showers and had little routines that made them both happy. Lance loved to have Keen wash his hair since Keen spent quality time scratching his scalp and smoothing the strands until they were shiny clean. Lance would have goose bumps on his shoulders from the hedonistic pleasure of being cared for. He, in turn, would scrub Keen's back, taking obvious delight in the moans Keen couldn't hold in.

These were familiar loving routines…things that made them a couple. They spent the rest of the time moving in and out of the spray, kissing and touching, laughing and joking. Everything was cleaned, and this time, knowing they were headed for the bed, they refrained from love games in the shower. They got out, dried each other lovingly, even slowly, savouring one another.

Keen took Lance's hand and led him around the room as he lit candle after candle. Most were scentless, some smelled subtly of pine trees and rain. Lance just took it all in, loving every minute of it. It was obvious from his glances and touches that he realised tonight was going to be something special and that Keen had gone to a lot of trouble for him.

They stood by the bed now, and Keen took Lance into his arms and held him, gently, reverently.

"Tonight is for you, Lance. For us, of course, but *my* wish is to make yours come true tonight." Keen looked into Lance's eyes and watched them get hot and melty-looking. Just the look he wanted.

"Then take me to bed, be wild and rough and hard and bossy. Take me hard then take me again, real sweet and tender like the other night. Is that asking too much?" Lance seemed hesitant now that he'd said exactly what he wanted.

"Crawl up there, right in the middle of the bed. I want you on your hands and knees. Ready for this?"

"Ready, willing, and able," Lance answered on his way up onto the bed and into position. He gave Keen an honest-to-God come-hither look over his shoulder. Keen laughed and followed him up onto the bed and began moving his hands over Lance's body, massaging deeply, making him feel it.

Keen started at Lance's shoulders, travelled over his back and ended by rubbing, pinching, and spreading Lance's cheeks, exposing his hole. He leant down and blew gently and chuckled at Lance's reaction. Bending further, he licked, lapped and sucked until Lance quivered and moaned, pushing back against him.

Keen started to reach for the lube and rubbers then realised they didn't need them anymore. He was so used to being careful all his adult life, but since they'd both gotten their results, they could be natural with each other. He changed his mind and said to Lance, "Get the lube, reach down and get yourself ready for me." He tried to sound rough like a good Dom should, but he just wasn't that way. He could give orders, but he was afraid they sounded more like heated requests.

Lance shivered at the words anyway and stretched for the lube. He looked over his shoulder at Keen with such a look of love in his eyes there was no mistaking it. Keen gave his own little shiver and watched as Lance followed orders and reached under and back to grease himself liberally, pushing in and out a few times before he rested his arms back on the bed and pushed back, open for Keen.

Keen wasted no time. He moved up until his knees were against Lance and held his hips still as he pushed right into him to the hilt. He echoed the groan that Lance started then he began to pound into his lover with everything he had. He held Lance's hips tight and rammed his cock into him over and over, hard and fast, loving the sounds he got in return. It wasn't long before he could tell that Lance was close to coming.

Keen reached down and took Lance's cock in one hand, and after a few tight squeezes, he felt Lance lose it. He let him go and took hold of both sides of Lance's hips again. He pounded into Lance a few more times then felt his own release beginning. Lance pushed back, giving to him now. He pushed in one final time and thought he saw lights as he came harder than he could ever remember. He collapsed onto Lance, and they went down, breathing hard and holding tight.

Eventually Lance nudged him, and they turned to settle into each other's arms, sharing kisses and sighs, trembles and nuzzles. Before long, Lance reached down and moved his hand between Keen's legs, getting just the response he seemed to be looking for. He was slow and languid in his movements, just like he'd said he wanted the next session of lovemaking to be. Keen could tell he wasn't in a hurry, so he let Lance just love on him a few minutes. He revelled in the fact that Lance made him feel so much.

Keen met Lance's request for tenderness as he moved him around on the bed just like he wanted him. Lance was now on his back looking up at Keen with anticipation and eagerness. Keen moved between Lance's legs and gently eased his hard cock back into him, never taking his eyes off Lance's. When he was seated tight inside him, he began to rotate his hips against Lance, giving him different sensations. He pulled out slowly, almost all the way, then eased back in, rotating his hips again. He could tell Lance loved it. He bent and took Lance's lips with his, pushing his tongue in and around. Lance raised his legs and clasp his hips with them, pulling him in and holding him still. Keen complied with the unsaid wish and they were connected in every way, his cock deep inside Lance, his tongue, too. Their eyes were open now and they looked steadily into each other's gaze, caught, held.

Lance pulled back a little and said, "Don't move…"

"Jesus, Lance. I'll try. You are so…God…hot, sexy, beautiful…mine."

"Right back at you, Keen, right back, all of it."

Neither knew how long they stayed that way nor who moved first. It may have been mutual, they were so in sync. The climax, when it came, was perfectly timed and together. It seemed to last forever, and Keen thought he had ever experienced anything like it before. They couldn't let go of each other. Hands touched and caressed, lips moved softly, kissed sweetly, and bodies were close and still convulsing gently now and then as they lay together.

Lance's stomach rumbled, and they both laughed a little.

"Hungry, baby?" Keen leaned up finally and looked down at Lance.

"Guess so. Can I tell you…well, I don't know if I *can* tell you what that meant to me. I've never felt anything like that. You make me so happy, Keen. That may sound just too, too sweet, but it's the only thing I can think of. You just make me happy."

"The feeling is mutual, Lance, believe that. Now let's take a quick shower, no playing, and go make your stomach happy." Keen laughed at Lance's expression.

"No playing?"

"Okay, a little playing. Then—"

"My surprise! Come on, let's go," Lance said, moving to the side of the bed, eager to get to the next step in whatever Keen had planned for tonight.

Within a few minutes, after minimal horseplay in the shower, they were both in the kitchen in comfy sweats, and Lance was trying to sneak tidbits of dinner before Keen could get it to the table.

"Behave. I'm trying to serve you dinner, goofy," Keen laughed as he pretended to smack Lance's hand when he reached around him.

"Can't help it. Starving. God, this smells good. You're the best, man. The best. What can I do to help?"

"Uh, get us something to drink and sit down. You're like the Energizer bunny."

"Hey, sometimes that's a good thing," Lance laughed as he pointed his finger at Keen.

"Gotta admit you're right there. Now, settle."

Lance got their drinks and settled, after scooting his chair closer to Keen's. The movement wasn't lost on Keen, who smiled to himself, loving it.

They shared the meal with soft talk and light laughter. It was perfect. They even managed to make it through dessert, which tonight was a special dark-chocolate cake with chocolate icing. They took turns feeding each other bites of the luscious treat.

Keen was surprised when Lance got up to start clearing the table and washing up.

"You don't have to do that. Leave it…" Keen started.

"Nope. Get it out of the way then we won't have to worry about it. I hope we have plans for later. Yeah?" Lance smiled as he kept moving quickly around the kitchen. Keen joined him, and in just a few minutes, the place was sparkling and empty.

Keen led Lance to the den where the beautiful, carved-wood box, with a bow on top, sat on the coffee table. Lance looked at him with uncertainty in his eyes.

"What did I miss? Why am I getting this...this night? Not that I'm not loving every single minute of it, but I feel like I should have something for you, too."

"I hope you do. Relax. Come on, sit down with me and open your gift. Oh, wait, do you know Jim Croce..." Keen started.

"Oh yeah, he was one of my Mom's favourites," Lance cut in. "She had on his stuff a lot at home. Dad liked the one about Leroy Brown, the baddest man in the whole damn town. Mom's was the one about time in a bottle. Why? You have it?" Lance looked over at Keen, questions in his eyes.

Keen leant over and pushed a button on a CD player and said, "Just listen to the words...like they're coming from me, okay?" He even said the words, softly, along with Jim on the CD, singing the words to Lance.

Lance made him extremely happy by paying close attention to the words, his eyes never leaving Keen's mouth as he sang to him. His eyes got a little misty, and he clearly caught all the words and meanings as Keen sang right into his heart. As the song ended, Keen reached for the box then handed it to Lance.

Lance took it into his hands, but before he opened it, he leant over and put his mouth to Keen's. There were tears in his eyes as he drew back and said, very quietly, "I love you, Keen, so much."

Keen's heart pounded hard as he leaned in and kissed Lance again.

"Open your gift first then the card, okay?" His voice was a little rough with emotion.

Lance sat back against the couch and took off the bow, then turned the box around and around, taking in all the beautiful carving on it.

"This is really beautiful, Keen," Lance said, finally taking the top off of it and setting it aside. He pulled out the vase, which was wrapped in several layers of tissue paper. His eyes got larger and larger as he unwrapped the layers and finally reached the vase.

He held it reverently in his hands and did Keen proud by reading every word of the song he'd just heard. He held it carefully in one hand and traced the etched words with the other. The words to the song were there, with Lance's name at the top and Keen's name at the bottom, like it was a letter to Lance.

Lance looked over at Keen again, his heart in his eyes. He was unashamed as he let Keen reach over and smooth the tears away for him. He turned the vase over slowly and took out the watch.

"Wow," he said, quietly, "this is beautiful."

"I hoped you'd like it," Keen said quietly, just as the moment warranted.

"It's time in a bottle, huh?"

"Yeah. Corny maybe, but…well…read the card, okay?" Keen was getting a little anxious.

Lance turned back, reached into the box and pulled out the card. He carefully set the vase down on the table then placed the watch on his arm, taking just a moment to admire it. Then he opened the card and read it. Twice.

Keen was to the side of him, so he saw Lance in profile. He watched as tears slipped down Lance's cheeks as he read the card again and again. Very slowly, Lance set the card on the table by the vase and turned to look at Keen. He leaned in and put his cheek against Keen's and whispered into his ear, "I love you, I love you, I love you. You *are* the love of my life. I've known it for a while, but was afraid to say it in case it might be too soon or…I don't know. I've never felt like this." His voice shook, but he kept on. "I didn't know how to act. I just know that everything in that letter is how I feel about you." His arms went around Keen's neck as he talked softly to him.

"If you're asking a question, the answer is yes. If you need anything, it's yours." Lance's voice grew stronger now. "Know this, I'm not unsure of my feelings for you. I. Love. You."

He ended by sliding his hands up and taking hold of Keen's face and giving him the sweetest, most emotional kiss Keen had ever experienced. They were both misty-eyed when it drew to an end, but neither seemed to care. They smiled at each other and wiped the moisture away and just sat.

"Hold me for a while?" Lance asked, love and need in his voice.

"Come here." Keen simply tightened his arms around Lance. "I love you so much. I'm offering you everything I have. I want you to live here with me. I want us to be together forever. I see us in the far distant future growing old together, caring for each other." He paused a moment and looked at Lance seriously. "Sometimes, I think you're too young to know your own mind," Keen could tell Lance wanted to interrupt, "but I know better. You're very grown up in your thoughts, your feelings, your work. I love everything about you." That was what Lance needed to hear. He kept hold of Lance, their faces pressed together, moving only a little in soft caresses.

"Maybe someday we might think about some kind of formal thing tying us together, if you'd like, but right now I want to make this our personal official commitment to each other. How do you feel about that?" He closed his eyes, waiting for Lance to answer.

Lance answered "The same way I've felt about everything that has happened since I walked in that door tonight. I'm the luckiest man on earth." There was no hesitation in Lance's voice as he continued, "I have everything I've ever wanted. The future is open and bright and filled with love and laughter and goodness. Yes, I would like to commit myself to this relationship with you. I'll do it now privately then later as publicly as you'd like. Whatever you want, wherever you go, just take me with you. Always."

"Looks like we're on the same page." Keen hadn't moved away from Lance, whose face was still pressed to his, with Lance's mouth by Keen's ear. He could feel Lance's lashes on his cheek as Lance blinked. Butterfly kisses, he thought.

"Same page, same feelings, same need to be together. Is there any better feeling?" Lance said, finally pulling his face back to look into Keen's eyes.

"Does feel good, doesn't it? I really think we've got what it takes to go the distance." Keen said, never taking his eyes off Lance's.

"I have no doubts. I've felt this for a while and I told myself you felt the same way, but having you say it, and like you did, means the world to me. I love you. Feels good to finally say it," Lance admitted, smiling.

"I love you. It does feel good to say it out loud and know it's accepted and returned. You've made my whole world better just with those words." Keen didn't mind admitting that he had needed to hear the words. "Our life together is pretty wonderful. This is just the icing on the cake for me."

"Thank you for going to all the trouble to make this special for me."

"I wanted to. You're special to me in so many ways. So," Keen looked at Lance and smiled, "happy, are you?"

"More than I can say. Do you have anything else planned?" Lance looked at Keen with mischief in his eyes.

"Uh, no. This is pretty much as far as I'd gotten. Why? You got plans now?" Keen could tell he did.

"Oh, yeah. You could say that. Wanna come with me? There's something I'd like to do, to you, with you, for you."

"There is, is there?" Keen smiled at him again.

"Yeah, anything I do will make me happy, too, so it's really for both of us. Come with me?" Lance stood and held his hand out to Keen.

"Always. I'll always come with you." Keen took the offered hand.

"Good answer."

Lance pulled Keen up into his arms and wrapped him right up in his long arms. He held tight, seeming to want to become a part of Keen right there. Keen helped. He put one arm around Lance's waist and the other around his neck and pulled. There bodies were flush against each other and their lips met in a ravenous kiss.

They had declared their love, agreed on a future together, cried together, and said tender, loving words to each other. Now they were eager to show that love in a different way. Since Lance had asked, Keen let him lead. Lance feasted on Keen's mouth, moving from nibbles and licks on Keen's full lips to mashing them and going deep inside with his tongue to sweep through Keen's mouth in an obvious attempt to become one with him.

"I'm shaking, I want you so much," Lance admitted as he finally eased his lips back and put his face against Keen's neck. His lips moved on Keen's skin as he talked.

"It all feels different now. I can remember saying to you once that being with you felt like…more. More everything than ever before, but now, it's even better. Thank you…for loving me." He ended and rubbed his face against Keen's shoulder, holding him so very close.

"Same page, remember. It *is* more. It's better. Love is the difference, isn't it, baby? I think you had a plan…" he reminded Lance, smiling as he felt Lance move against him, rubbing their hips together.

"Yeah. I want to put that vase in our bedroom. I want to spend some time in the shower with you, taking care of you. Will you let me…just do for you, play with you, make you feel good?" How Lance could doubt that Keen would agree was a mystery.

"Anything. I'm all yours. Literally. Anything you do will make me feel good. I'm already so happy I could dance on air."

Lance just smiled at him, taking his hand and leading him back to their room. Keen went happily, knowing he would love what came next. Lance stopped by the bed and pushed gently on Keen's shoulder, urging him to sit on the edge. Keen sat. He looked up at Lance, waiting to see what he would do next. He didn't have long to wait.

Lance stepped in close, between Keen's legs and began to ease his shirt over his head. He flipped it to the corner and turned back to Keen. He smoothed over Keen's head with both hands, touching, moulding, smoothing. He seemed very serious about his task, taking time to massage and caress every inch. Keen soaked up the attention, staying quiet, as Lance seemed to want.

Keen sat still as Lance moved down to his neck and shoulders with the same tender ministrations. Keen caught on. There would not be a place that Lance did not claim. He was fine with that. He became the puppet that Lance controlled with a touch, push, or pull. He stood on command, and Lance divested him of his pants and he sat again upon silent request. Lance just leant into him to force him down onto the bed. Keen had long since begun to quiver at the touches and the care shown by Lance.

Lance, literally left not a spot on Keen's body that wasn't caressed and worshipped in his own way. Lance ignored the very hard and leaking cock that stood eager, awaiting attention. By the time he had moved all the way from the top to the bottom of Keen's feet and back, then turned him and done the same to the other side, Keen was moaning and near begging. He didn't though. He knew this was important to Lance. Keen wanted to let him have his way, though it was nearly killing him.

He couldn't help the shout when Lance spread his cheeks and began to lave his hole, still slow and gentle. He pushed up to make it easier for Lance. He was afraid he was going to come just like that. His whole body was sensitised to the point of glorious agony. Lance's tongue was working his hole and his hand was gently manipulating his balls, squeezing and rolling them as they tightened and pulled up as he got closer and closer.

Suddenly, Lance pulled back, took Keen's hips and flipped him over again. He bent to take Keen into his mouth, taking nearly the whole length of him at once. The heat and suction had Keen making the neediest, sexiest noises. He couldn't help it. He leaned up and watched as Lance took his final bit of sanity and strength.

He gave it all up and nearly lost it as Lance began to hum and move up and down, giving the best head he'd ever experienced. Keen jerked as Lance reached down to his balls again, caressing and rolling them. Seconds later, he reached behind Keen and pushed one finger into his hole as he pulled off his dick and held it with the other hand. He pushed his tongue into the slit at the tip and Keen nearly passed out as he came like he never had before. He tried to stay up on his elbows and watch as Lance swallowed him down. Lance was flushed and sweating as he kept at Keen until he was totally wasted. Keen had fallen to the bed and was trying to hold on to the covers as he tried to get a full breath.

"My God, that was..." Keen paused, looking for a word and settling on, "...fantastic."

"I was inspired." Lance admitted, smiling up at Keen. He crawled up to lie beside Keen and snuggled in, kissing and caressing, softly now, easing Keen into a state of near oblivion.

"I love you." Just a plain bald statement. Keen watched as Lance took the words into his heart and felt Lance wrap his arms tighter around him. He was almost dozing when he suddenly had a thought that had him sitting right up. Lance was lying very still and obviously taking great care to not let Keen feel how hard he was and how much he needed relief. This had so clearly been just for Keen.

Oh, I don't think so, Keen thought.

Keen looked down at Lance, who was turning to see why Keen had moved away. Keen reached to take Lance's cock in his hand and moved up and down it for a few seconds.

"Keen, oh..."

"Yeah, oh. What you just did was absolutely wonderful and I loved every minute of it, but I think there's something I need to take care of here." Keen took note of the way Lance was beginning to breathe deeper and starting to quiver as he continued to caress him. "This is a night for both of us. I'd say it's your turn."

"Yippee…" Lance managed to get out as he pushed up into Keen, forcing him back down and the two were rolling across the bed, laughing and touching each other. Keen enjoyed the play but kept his goal in mind, getting Lance off as beautifully as he'd been loved.

In keeping with Lance's slow lovemaking, Keen followed suit and took his time with Lance. He started as Lance had with his hands in Lance's hair, smoothing, caressing, massaging. He could tell by the look on Lance's face how he was enjoying it. He continued and, without really trying to copy exactly, his route did seem to follow the one Lance had set on him. He teased, tasted, and fully memorised Lance.

"You like this, don't you, baby?" Keen asked, his lips just then against the join of Lance's thigh and groin, making Lance shiver at the sensation and the words. "You like slow and soft and teasing. I can tell…you took great joy in rocking my world. I loved it," Keen kept his lips moving as he talked quietly to Lance, keeping him eager to hear more, feel more.

"I like making you hum. You sound so sexy."

"Love you, Keen, love you," Lance gasped out, turning to allow Keen access to his hip as Keen reached to turn him a little.

"That makes me happier than I can tell you," Keen said, smiling up at him, "I'll just have to show you." Now, he reached back over to take Lance in his mouth and worked him slow and long, reading Lance perfectly. He knew right when to tighten his hold and suck hard, reaching down to give Lance's balls a tweak then he just held on and swallowed fast. He looked up past the bellowing flat stomach to see Lance blinking slowly and still humming a little.

"There's my guy. I like that look on you," Keen said, climbing up to lie beside him, taking Lance into his arms and turning so Lance was lying across him a little, Lance's head resting on his shoulder. He liked feeling the deep breaths coming across his neck. He reached up to caress Lance's head and neck, loving on him a little, easing him a little.

"I may never move again," Keen heard the words against his neck and smiled as Lance went on. "I could stay like this forever. I really could."

"I hear you. I'm feeling pretty satisfied right now myself. Could use a big old sloppy kiss, though," he hinted, pulling on Lance's hair a little to get his mouth within range.

* * * *

Keen woke and wondered what time it was. Not wanting to wake Lance, he edged his arm up and checked his watch. They'd left the bathroom light on and the door partially open so there was low light, enough to see it was 3:45 a.m. He sighed deeply and thought about happiness for a moment. He'd never really been *un*happy. His life had been pretty good. But now...*now* he knew what real happiness was all about.

He turned his head to look at the living breathing reason for the richness of his feelings. His eyes grew wide as he saw that Lance wasn't asleep either. His beautiful lover was on his side, head propped on his hand, eyes steady on Keen.

"Hey," Keen said, his surprise at finding Lance awake evident.

"Hey." Lance didn't move, just kept looking at Keen.

"Hon? What's up? You okay?" Keen turned more towards Lance and gazed at him as he waited for his answer.

"No," Lance said, quietly.

"No? No, you're not okay?" Keen became concerned. Was Lance sick? Should he—

Lance chuckled and leaned towards Keen. "Relax. I'm not okay. I'm thrilled, happy, ecstatic. You're more than my wildest dreams."

Keen opened his arms and pulled Lance against him, loving him so much.

"How long have you been awake?" he murmured, yawning.

"Haven't gone to sleep. Was just watching you, loving you. I've been trying to take it all in…that you love me…as much as I love you. That's just so big."

"Believe it. You're my man," Keen nuzzled his face into Lance's neck and inhaled.

"I am," Lance started then shivered and ended with satisfaction, "your…your man. And you're mine."

"Oh, yeah." Keen's lips moved over the top of Lance's shoulder, dropping sweet, sucking kisses along it before heading back for Lance's neck.

"Keen?" Lance said and waited.

"Yeah?"

"Thank you for last night. It was just beautiful, all of it. I love that you planned all that for me. The supper and the gifts and…you sang to me." There was a sort of wonder in his voice as he remembered the beauty in those special moments.

"You liked that, huh?"

"Loved it. You have a beautiful voice. Will you sing for me again some time?" Lance's eyes lit up as he waited to see what Keen would say.

"Maaaaay...beeeeee," Keen drawled and tightened his arms around Lance.

Lance laughed and pulled hard. Keen went with it and found himself over on top of Lance, looking down at his smiling face.

"Well, hello there. Something I can help you with?"

"Fuck me," Lance said. Keen's eyes flared at the words and he dropped his head, taking Lance's mouth hard and fast. Lance opened, and Keen thrust inside, sweeping through like he'd gone for weeks without sustenance. His tongue catalogued Lance's mouth, missing nothing. He moved over teeth, pushing against them, liking the scrape against his tongue. He slid over gums and got up close and personal with the roof of Lance's mouth. He played tag with Lance's tongue, stroking and tangling with it, sucking on it.

"Mmph!" Lance managed and dragged his hands down Keen's sides, grabbing his hips and dragging them hard against his own. Their cocks brushed, and two gasps were heard. They settled in and began to move in a fabulous rhythm. Before long they were both close to losing it.

"Keen, oh...stop...please...I want..." Lance was nearly incoherent, but obviously sure about what he wanted.

Keen pushed hard against Lance's hips and held still, breathing hard, afraid he was going to come right then. It thrilled him that Lance didn't hesitate to tell him what he wanted from him. He breathed deeply through his nose and finally felt he could relax and ease away from Lance.

He pulled back, looked down and smiled into Lance's eyes.

"Turn over, baby. I want in that fine, fine ass."

Lance blushed a little, but lost no time flipping over. He even threw in a little shimmy as he settled, making his cheeks jiggle a little.

Keen actually made a growling noise at the obvious invitation. God, he loved this man!

* * * *

Keen came in the front door carrying a duffle bag from the gym and a laptop from the office. He wasn't expecting Lance home for a couple of hours. He was surprised when he smelled something wonderful cooking. He had made it clear to Phoebe that she was not there to cook for them. He and Lance usually handled the meals with her pitching in a little here and there. What was she up to?

He put his things away and followed his nose to the kitchen.

"Phoebe, love, I've told you that—oh, hello. Not Phoebe." He stopped his words and his steps and just looked at Lance. Just looked at the man. His man. He was just gorgeous, standing there shirtless, his sweats hanging low on his hips, barefooted, with his hair still wet from a shower. Lord, Keen wanted him a piece of that.

"What's up, baby? You're home early…and cooking. Where's Phoebe?" He had to ask, 'cause he wanted to just go over and devour the man from head to toe, just gobble him right up. Best not done in the kitchen with company liable to walk in.

"Welcome home, honey." Lance finally turned to face him, and Keen's jaw dropped.

"Lance! When did you... Oh wow. Does that hurt?"

Lance had a tiny tattoo on his left pec, right over his heart. Keen walked over for a closer look. He'd noticed it right away because it was a little red around the tat, obviously new. As he drew nearer, he saw that it was the letters, KDT. Keen Dale Thomas. Oh man, his lover had *his* initials tattooed on his chest, over his heart.

Oh, wait. This whole scene seemed a little familiar. Uh, huh. Like a scene from Phoebe's ninth and final book.

"You like it?" Lance looked hesitant.

"I love it. I especially love that you took it right from Phoebe's last book. Cool, Lance." He reached out to touch, gently, the area around the letters. He smiled as Lance shivered and moved closer to him. It was really very small and neat, not at all gaudy or too noticeable. It was just there for him, he knew, and it meant so much.

"I loved what you did for me that night...when...when you told me you loved me. That was special, really special, to me. I wanted to do something just for you. Just to show you how much I love you and want to be with you from now on. It's a little sore, but it'll be better in a couple of days. It's just little." Lance started to turn back to the stove.

"Yeah, it *is* little, but it's...it's huge, baby. Huge." Keen bent and so, so tenderly kissed the letters over Lance's heart, causing Lance to shiver and groan.

"Where's Phoebe?" Keen whispered.

"At Sandy's...again. She knows I did it. She said she approved." Lance wiggled in Keen's grasp as he moved his lips over Lance's chest, nuzzling the other pec and taking the nipple into his mouth and teasing it.

"No doubt she does," Keen chuckled against Lance's neck as he moved up to nibble along his collarbone.

"Mmm, feels good, Keen." Lance couldn't help moving closer, showing how badly he wanted to feel more of Keen against him.

"S'posed to. Uh, whatcha cookin'? Can it wait…say for about an hour or…longer?"

"Mm-hmm." Lance was able to mumble as Keen walked him backwards to the stove, and he twisted to turn it off as they headed for the bedroom. Halfway there, Keen detoured, and they ended up in the den where Keen had presented Lance with *his* gift that night. Lance looked surprised but willing as Keen drew him towards the big couch.

Lance laughed when Keen pushed him backwards from the end of the couch. Down he went with Keen following to land on top of him. They both chuckled and rearranged arms and legs to get comfortable.

Just as the chuckles slowed down and silence reigned, Lance spoke up quietly, "Keen?"

"Yeah, baby?" Keen pulled his head from Lance's neck to look into his eyes.

"Is this too good? I mean, it's everything I ever hoped for and I'm so happy. I'm afraid something is going to be taken away 'cause it's not fair for it to be so perfect. Sounds stupid, I know. I was just thinking about how good it all is…" Lance looked steadily at Keen as he expressed his fears.

"Yeah, sometimes, I think the same thing, but whatever happens, we'll face it together. I know you worry about this. If there are problems ahead, and there may well be, we're twice as strong, right?" Keen leaned to kiss Lance quickly then waited for his answer.

"Definitely. Together. Ignore me. I just get goofy," Lance said, closing his eyes and sighing.

"I love you goofy. I love you sexy. I love you…oh don't let me get started. The list would go on way past suppertime. I think I had a plan for us. Refresh my memory…" He laughed down at Lance, looking at his mouth and going for the smouldering eyes.

Lance laughed at him and brought his arms up to hug him tight around the neck. He rocked back and forth with Keen in his arms.

"Love you," he mumbled, squeezing Keen.

"Love you," Keen replied and pushed back, putting his hands on the couch on either side of Lance's head. He looked down and playfully put his tongue out and leaned slowly to touch the tip to Lance's lips, top, bottom, and across the seam. When Lance opened, he pulled his tongue back. Lance's came out and he hummed a little. That's what he wanted. He touched his tongue to Lance's and there followed a lively game of tag. They teased and played and before long, breathing deepened and they settled, feasting on each other's mouths.

Keen soon slid down a little to put his lips to Lance's chest, near the new tattoo.

"Hurt?" he whispered, as he moved around it, not wanting to cause Lance anything near pain.

"Nah, tender, itchy. Don't stop." Lance put his hands around Keen's head, moving them through his hair and holding him where he was. "You like it, huh?" he asked, smiling.

"Understatement. Blew me away when I saw it. You just keep on surprising me," Keen said, his lips against Lance's pec. He loved the taste of Lance's skin, had come to crave it, actually. He felt he could pick his man out of a line-up by taste and smell alone. The thought made him smile.

"What?" Lance could evidently feel the smile on his lips.

"Nothing, I just love the way you smell…and taste." Keen playfully put his teeth to the other side of Lance's chest and pretended to take a big bite. Lance pushed his hips up against him and groaned.

"Oh, hello. I think you liked that," Keen teased and moved up and did the same thing against the top of his shoulder and smiled when Lance shivered.

"Oh, my. I just love finding out new things about you. Wish you'd told me about this. You just lie there and let me see what else you like…" Keen set to work with a dedicated mind.

He found several places that made Lance moan and wiggle and when he took a playful nip right beside Lance's leaking cock, he felt Lance come up from the couch and give a little yelp, just shaking for him.

"Just look at you," Keen said, "my sexy love. I'm gonna make you come just like this."

Keen moved off Lance and knelt on the floor beside the couch. When Lance tried to protest at losing the weight of him, Keen put his hand up to ease him back down.

"S'okay, baby. I'll be back up there, but first, turn just a little. That's it, I want to play with you."

"Does that make me your boy toy?" Lance asked, lying back and looking at Keen from under his lashes.

"Oh, definitely. But, I'll be yours, too…later, okay?" Keen laughed and leant back down to spend some more time making Lance squirm.

"Yeah, later. My turn. Oh!" He jumped, shivered, and then settled, obviously looking forward to later.

Epilogue

Keen went to Sandy for help. His heart was breaking because he couldn't reach Lance. It hurt that he couldn't be the one to ease Lance's pain. He was grieving, too. They all were. But Phoebe's death had hit Lance the hardest.

Luckily, they'd had more than three years with her. Even luckier was the fact that she had died in her sleep one night. Keen was so glad that Lance had not been forced to watch her in pain or illness, wasting away as she'd had to watch with her Ally.

The service for Phoebe was more than two weeks ago, and Lance had not been able to face her death. Keen was at his wits' end. He had loved her immensely and hated that she was gone. He would be forever grateful for knowing her and spending those years with her.

He had tried talking to Lance several times about how she had loved him and would not want him to be so broken up, but it fell on deaf ears. Lance was closed off. They still slept in the same bed, cooked, ate, worked, and so on. It was just done with very little talking and no joy at all in living.

"Sandy, honey, what am I going to do? He's just existing. He won't talk about her or cry or get angry. He just goes through days like a zombie. I knew he'd be upset. I just never thought it would do this to him."

"He doesn't know how to handle his grief."

He ran his hand over his head and grabbed the back of his aching neck. "Hell, we're all having a hard time. But we all expected it sooner or later. How do I make him see that she had a wonderful life and that it should be celebrated, not mourned?"

"I know, hon. Kale and I have talked about it, too. Have you gone to her grave with him, or suggested he go alone to tell her goodbye?" At his nod, she shook her head, and said, "I'm lost. He's working, though, right?"

"Yeah, he goes in and works. We sleep in the same bed, but…well…the first night he let me hold him all night, but he didn't sleep. Since then, he just turns to the wall and crosses his arms over his chest. We don't shower together anymore, and let me tell you, *that* hurts. I feel selfish being hurt that he isn't turning to me to help him through this. How crazy is that?" He was sitting on the couch in living room, and he dropped his head into his hands and scrubbed at his face.

He was fighting tears. He'd lost Phoebe and now it felt like he was losing Lance, too. Sandy sat beside him and rubbed his back and shoulder.

"Mommy," a sweet little voice said from the doorway, "whassa matta wif Unca Kee?"

Keen's head came up and he twisted to see Phoebe Ann standing there, looking like an angel with her blond curls and bright blue eyes. He held out his arms and she ran to him. He swept her up onto his lap and hugged her to him. She was the joy of all their lives. She was sweet, bright, and beautiful, like her namesake.

"Hi, baby. You been nappin'?" he said, smoothing her hair. His heart turned over as she laid her head on his chest and snuggled into him.

"You sad, Unca Kee?" she whispered, reaching up to pat his face with her little fingers.

"Not any more, darling. You've made it all better," Keen said, looking at Sandy and nodding. It was true, he realised.

"I am," he said, looking at Sandy. "I am better. I'm not going to give up. I'll smother him with love and hugs and tenderness until he breaks and cries and comes back to me. No more of this hiding his pain. Thanks, girls."

He kissed the top of Phoebe's little head and passed her to her mother. He leant over and kissed Sandy, too, before heading out the door and back to his house where he was going to get it done. He would force Lance to face his grief and get it all out and find his lover again. They should be helping each other through this, and he was going to make it happen.

* * * *

When Lance came in the door that afternoon he paused. The blinds were drawn again, and he could smell supper cooking. So Keen was home and had been busy in the kitchen. He dropped his bag and headed down the hall to the bedroom to take a shower. He wasn't ready to see Keen right now. When he got to the door he saw a note on it that said, "Nope. Come straight to the den, please."

What the hell? A summons to the den? What was going on here? He didn't want to go in there and have Keen try to talk to him again. He wanted to go and shower and hide—hide in the bedroom and not…not have to think about…

"Please," came from the end of the hall. He turned and there was Keen. He wore an old pair of sweats, no shirt, no shoes. For a second, Lance thought about how sexy he looked. Just for a second. He stood still, then, dropped his head, not wanting to look at Keen any more.

He knew he'd been a shit for the past weeks. He'd treated Keen like crap, and he didn't deserve kindness. He just felt…what? What did he feel?

"Lance…please…I need you." Now that was unfair. Straight out unfair. He tried hard and was able to lift his head. Keen still stood there, waiting. Lance didn't know what to do. He wanted to…to hide. But he couldn't ignore Keen. He couldn't continue to ignore him. But…it was so hard.

"I know. I know it's hard," Keen said.

Had he said that out loud or was Keen reading his mind? Didn't matter. He wasn't going to be able to ignore him. He was going to have to go to him and listen to whatever he wanted to say. He owed him that.

He walked slowly to the end of the hall where Keen waited. He stopped right in front of him, still with his head down. He watched Keen's right hand come out and take his left and pull him just that little bit farther, enough so that they touched. His head now rested on Keen's shoulder. He stood, afraid to move, not willing to go that minute distance more. He felt a shudder pass through Keen's body then heard a sob right by his ear.

Oh hell. He jerked his head around and bumped into the side of Keen's face. There were tears rolling down his cheek, and he wasn't even trying to hide the sobs now. His shoulders shook and he made big gulping noises as if he were trying to stop the sobs, but they just kept coming. Lance couldn't stand it. He put his hands around Keen and pulled him to him, tight. He just held on and pushed his face into Keen's neck. He didn't know what to do.

"I'm...sorry..." Keen said against his shoulder. But he couldn't stop crying, it seemed. He just held on and cried his heart out as Lance held him there in the hall. Lance finally moved a bit, turning Keen and putting his back against the hall wall. He leaned into him and the dam burst. He gave in.

Keen held tight as Lance let out a scream of rage and pain. His arms grasped Lance strongly as his body began to shake and shudder. Great sobs racked him, and he pushed his face into Keen's neck like he'd never come up again. They both stood in the hall, leaning on the wall across from the room where Phoebe had lived and cried their hearts out.

How long they stood there, Keen didn't know. After a while, he pushed a little and began to walk, pulling Lance with him until they were at the bedroom door. He pushed it open and drew Lance to the bed. No words were spoken, and the tears weren't over. Keen drew Lance's shirt over his head, bent and removed his shoes. Then he pushed, and Lance dropped down onto the bed and just sat there. Keen pushed more, and Lance turned and lay down.

Keen crawled up beside him and took him back into his arms and wouldn't let go when Lance tried to pull away.

No more hiding. He crushed Lance to his chest and held him.

"Please, I need you," Keen said, again. Lance settled.

It was hours before either moved. Their sobs finally quieted and the tears finally stopped. They were still plastered against each other. Neither slept. Keen lay there, thinking about Phoebe and love and caring and pain and death and hope and life and what it would be like now. He knew Lance thought the same things. He'd cried as much for Lance's pain, as for his own. No words were spoken. But they never let go of each other.

Sometime in the middle of the night, Keen rolled off the bed went to the bathroom. When he returned, he had a warm washcloth in his hand. He leant over and smoothed it over Lance's face, neck and shoulders. He pulled back the covers and crooked his finger at Lance, telling him to get under them. Lance rolled, and Keen's heart flipped when Lance opened his arms to him, inviting him in. He sent the cloth sailing into the bathroom and settled into Lance's arms, and they slept the rest of the night like that.

The next day, Keen was up early. He called Hammer and told him Lance wouldn't be in that day, Friday. Hammer said it was about time he took a day. Keen hoped Lance wouldn't be upset with him. He thought they both needed the day. He went in and dumped last night's supper in the trash and started breakfast. When it was ready, he went to wake Lance.

As he walked into the bedroom, he heard the shower going. He waited for Lance to finish and was there with a towel when he stepped out. Lance jerked in surprise. He looked worn out and ragged. He reached for the towel.

"Let me. Please," Keen said quietly. Lance dropped his arms and stood, head down. He still had a long way to go.

Keen dried him off matter-of-factly with no playing. He pulled him into the bedroom and stood as Lance dressed. He then took Lance's hand and pulled him to the kitchen.

When Lance saw the cinnamon rolls on the counter, he stopped dead in his tracks and his eyes got huge. He looked at Keen angrily.

"What? No."

"Yes. Yes, Lance. Sit down," Keen said, pushing him towards the table and chairs. He took the coffee and plate of rolls and set them on the table. "Please, sit down with me."

"What are you doing? I can't... I don't want..."

"What? You don't want to eat the rolls because they're her recipe? You don't want to talk about her? You don't want to remember her? You don't want to think about her and how much she loved you?" Keen was on a roll now. "You don't want to be happy, because she's gone? You don't want to see your niece? You don't want to ever smile again, be happy again, make love again? You think it's honouring her memory to live in a vacuum?"

Lance shook, Keen thought, due to anger and pain, shame and grief. He clearly hated what Keen said because it was all true. Keen figured Lance was thinking all of that and feeling like a fool because of it.

"What do you want from me?" Lance yelled.

"Finally! I'm glad you asked." Keen sat down across from him. He deliberately reached out and took a roll and bit into it. He nearly choked on it. The lump in his throat didn't leave room for the bite to go down. He reached for the coffee, hoping that would help. Not. He forced another bite into his mouth. He didn't expect the tears that rolled down his cheeks as he continued to eat the roll, but he didn't try to stop them, either. He never took his eyes off Lance, who watched him in dawning horror.

"Why are you doing this?" Lance asked brokenly, wiping tears from his own eyes.

"I'm hurting. I've lost Phoebe and now you. I loved her as much as you did, Lance, and I miss her just as much." He wiped at the tears and leant back, crossing his arms over his chest, trying to hold himself together. "But I always thought when she left us we'd have each other. We'd help each other through it. With the love we had for each other, we would be able to make it through the grief of losing her. But, you closed up. You won't let me in. You don't need me or won't admit it if you do. You have no idea how much it hurts me that you won't hurt with me."

"I'm sorry...I...you're right...I just...I don't know how..." Lance trailed off, as if knowing there wasn't anything he could say that would make it right. "Do you want me to leave?" he asked quietly.

"What? No! *Hell,* no! Lance, I'm saying I need you, not that I want you to go anywhere. Are you listening? Don't *ever* think I want you to leave. Please...oh, I'm not doing *any*thing right if you think that. How could you think that?"

Lance shrugged. "I just keep hurting you, making things worse."

"So you think maybe we could try to work together to make things better? Can we talk now? Phoebe was someone who deserves to be remembered with love and laughter and...and rolls." He pushed the plate a little towards Lance. "Come on, baby. They should make you happy. How many pans has she made for us over the years? She taught me how to make them. I'll show you. And your niece has her name. You have to love her for it, not avoid her because of it. Can you tell me why this has hit you so hard? I want to help. I know it's selfish of me to want to be the one to help you, but I can't help it. It kills me that you won't share your pain with me. I feel like I'm failing you somehow." Keen hated admitting it, but he would admit to anything to get Lance back.

"No. It's not you. I don't know, Keen. Yes, I miss her, and I know we all do. But, it *scared* me. I sat at that funeral and thought about what she had meant to me then I thought about all of you and how much you all mean to me and I got scared. I looked down that pew at church and saw everything I loved so much and I was almost frozen with fear."

Lance looked at Keen with so much hurt in his eyes that Keen almost came up out of his chair, but he let Lance go on.

"What if something happened to you, I thought? Or Sandy? Or little Phoebe? Oh God, that beautiful little doll. I've been scared out of my mind. I just wanted to hide. I admit it. It was unfair of me. You needed me, and I let you down. I'll never forget that I hurt you like that. I don't know what to do to make it better. It was fear. Just fear. It was easier to hide than to face the fact I was scared to *death* of losing you, any of you." He ducked his head. "You're in love with a big coward."

"I'm in love with *you*. I love you with my whole heart." Keen stood and went to stand by Lance's chair. "Honey, this is just a bump in the road. You're not a coward. Your heart was broken, and you didn't know how to deal with it, so you allowed your grief to turn into fear for other loved ones. That's a sign of a really big heart, which I knew anyway. What do you want to do right now, right this minute?"

Lance looked up into Keen's eyes and his own filled with tears again. He scooted back his chair and pushed up into Keen's waiting arms. He threw his arms around Keen's neck and held on. He sniffed and turned his face so he could kiss Keen's neck. He was shaking.

"I love you, Lance. Always will. Relax, baby. We talked about this before, didn't we? That someday there would be bad stuff. We've had a charmed relationship up to this. Everything just fell into place, and we were so very happy. Life isn't like that, is it? There are hard things to have to face, too. It's being able to face it together that makes it bearable. The strength of our love for each other is what will get us through this and anything else life throws at us. Now tell me, what do you want?"

Lance cleared his throat, took a deep breath, and said, "I'm hungry. I want some Phoebe rolls. I want to go back to bed with you and make love 'til we can't move a muscle, but I have to go to work. I want to go see Phoebe Ann and just hold her and laugh with her and tickle her and play horsie with her." He began to smile a little as his heart seemed to open again, thanks to Keen's persistence. He went on, able now to voice his thoughts and needs. "I want to read all Phoebe's books over again, starting with number one and going all the way through. I want to honour her. I want to talk about her and remember her and be happy that I knew her as long as I did. I want to be happy that we found her and made her life better and made her happy. She died happy, didn't she?" he finally ended.

"Yes, darling. She died a happy woman. She had her lover most of her life then she had a whole new family. She left lots of money to cancer research, lots to her sweet Phoebe Ann and set it up to where the proceeds from future sales of her books will be used however the four of us deem appropriate. We'll have to think about that, okay?"

Keen began to massage Lance's shoulders and neck, feeling the tight tension ease a little. Finally.

"What could we do that would make her proud? Maybe something to do with the cancer kids at the hospitals? You can help me with that...Sandy, too. So, give me a lip-smacking kiss and let's eat Phoebe rolls. Oh, and you don't have to go in to work today. I called in sick for you."

"Thank you. And thank you for making me face this. I feel stupid now for being so...helpless. Mostly I'm sorry for not turning to you. Forgive me?"

"I'll let you make it up to me. I think somewhere in there you said something about making love 'til we're too tired to move. Count me in. I've missed you. Come here, kiss." Keen put his hands on either side of Lance's face and held him still for the much-needed kiss. The emotion that had built up over the last few weeks was released in that long sweet kiss.

They stood and swayed together, Lance's arms tight around Keen's neck, and Keen holding Lance's head still as he dipped and licked and swept through his mouth. They touched tongues gently and moved back and forth from mouth to mouth, breath ratcheting up a notch as they began to forget everything but their love for each other. Finally, Lance's stomach growled loudly, and they both jumped. They split apart, laughing.

Keen reached down for a roll and put it to Lance's mouth. Lance took a bite and closed his eyes, clearly savouring it, as if remembering the woman who'd first made them for him. Keen took a bite from the other side then turned and sat down, pulling Lance into his lap. They ate the whole plate of rolls and drank all the coffee.

Keen started by talking about meeting Phoebe and how feisty she was and how proud they were when they all went to the launch party for her books. Lance hit upon her work with the young cancer patients at the hospital where Sandy worked. They both smiled as they remembered her joy in Sandy's baby and how thrilled she'd been that Sandy named the child after her.

Keen knew that this was what they both had needed. This cleansing, healing discussion of how much they loved her and how much she had meant to them all. They finished the food, cleaned up and headed back to the bedroom.

They made good on the promise to love each other to the point of exhaustion. Lance was eager to make up to Keen for hurting him the past weeks, and Keen was eager to prove that he had forgiven him. They were both sweaty and glowing as they lay, trying to get their breath back.

Lance finally turned and looked down at Keen, saying, "I want to go back to the club this weekend. Remember taking Phoebe and how she loved watching the dancing and the couples and how she was the life of the party when that group from the publishing house saw her and knew her. She held court like a queen, which was fitting, considering where we were." Lance laughed remembering her delight in being with their friends.

"Baby, I am so glad you're beginning to be able to remember her with laughter and love, not sadness. You know how she was. She'd have jumped up and slapped you if she'd seen you lately, now wouldn't she?" Keen teased him.

"Yep. She was such a feisty, wonderful person. God, I love you."

"Me?" Keen didn't get the connection.

"Without you, I'd never have known her, never have had a home to bring her to, and you know the rest. I'm just glad I met and fell in love with you. You've changed my life, Keen."

"Same to ya, Lance." Keen reached to trace the letters KDT on Lance's chest. It's a wonder he hadn't rubbed it off by now. He loved it so much.

"Can we see if Sandy, Kale, and Phoebe Ann can go out tonight? Or maybe we could cook out for them over here? What do you think? It's time I came out of hiding, thanks to you." Lance put his lips on Keen's chin and began to take little nibbling kisses all along his jaw.

"Sounds like a plan. But first, I want more of you. We've got lots of time to make up. I need my lover back, my insatiable, inventive, sexy lover." Keen laughed as Lance blushed. He pulled him over on top of him, reaching down behind him to caress Lance's rounded cheeks. Keen traced down the centre of them and grinned when Lance spread for him. He teased him with soft touches and gentle strokes.

"More," Lance begged, wiggling to get their cocks lined up and brushing against each other.

"Yes," Keen answered. He pushed up against Lance and reached for his mouth at the same time. Keen tightened his arms around Lance and turned him so that now *he* was on top. Keen pulled back and looked down at the love of his life. He smiled and bent to put his tongue to the letters on Lance's chest. He moved his mouth over the area, licking and nipping Lance's nipples, making him cry out. It had been too long.

Keen took his time and left no place untouched, unloved. He moved all the way down the left side and up the right 'til he stopped and spent a long, loving time in the middle. He took Lance into his mouth and sucked hard, loving the sounds he heard over his head. Keen pulled back a little and licked up and down the length of Lance's cock, down to and surrounding his balls.

He laved them and took them into his mouth to roll them and push them against the roof of his mouth, loving the shudders and sighs that got. His fingers slid back and teased Lane's hole, pushing in and moving gently. Keen raised his head to ask for the lube and found it right there in Lance's hand, waiting for him. Smart man.

Keen managed to get Lance prepared and before long he was straddling him, then kneeling between his legs and spreading him wide open. He eased up and put his dick right there and pushed. He filled Lance with one long stroke. He was still for a moment, savouring the sensations. Lance's muscles squeezed him, and Keen began to move in and out, slowly at first, then fast and hard. He looked down and saw Lance watching him with such love evident in his eyes that Keen paused. He had to lean down and take a kiss.

Lance put his hands on Keen's butt cheeks and held him tightly inside him as he kissed him. Then Keen eased back a little, and his tongue matched the rhythm of his cock. Keen heard Lance whimpering with the strong feelings Keen knew were swamping him. He held on and rode it out. Keen reached down to take Lance's cock into his hand and with only a few strokes Lance came hard.

"Keen…Keen…love you," Lance managed to say, trying to keep his eyes open, but he needed to close them. He opened them again just as Keen let out a loud sigh and began to pump into him, coming deep inside him. Lance smiled up at Keen as he closed his eyes again. He managed to put his arms around Keen when he felt him ease out and lie beside him.

"Love you, Lance. Sleep now, baby." Keen's heart was full.

* * * *

"Unca Lace, wher' ya *been*? I miss you." Phoebe Ann ran to him and laughed when he picked her up and swung her around. When he stopped, she settled into his arms, hers around his neck. She laid her head on his shoulder and reached up to pat his face.

"You been sad, too, Unca Lace?"

Smart little thing, he thought.

"Yeah, baby, but I'm better now."

"Unca Kee make you better?" she asked and didn't know why everyone laughed.

"Yes, he did, Phoebe. Unca Kee made me all better."

"Good. I love Unca Kee." It obviously made perfect sense to her.

"Me, too, hon. Me, too."

About the Author

AKM Miles loves reading the M/M genre and decided to write what she loves. Early authors, read years ago in this area, were not as much interested in love, storyline, and character development, as those that she has found recently. Thrilled with the new works, AKM set out to make a career in this field. You can expect there to be a happy ending every time. You can expect for the two to find each other and choose to be together fairly early on, and then face conflicts, trials, and experiences as a couple. AKM prefers that over going back and forth over whether the love is returned or not. She loves to throw children in the mix, along with pets and wacky and wonderful friends. Hopefully, readers will love the emotional love stories that fill her head and spill onto her computer.

AKM Miles loves to hear from readers. You can find her contact information, website details and author profile page at http://www.total-e-bound.com.

Total-E-Bound Publishing

www.total-e-bound.com

Take a look at our exciting range of literagasmic™
erotic romance titles and discover pure quality
at Total-E-Bound.